DOLLARS FOR THE REAPER

Bounty-hunter Jonathan Grimm was 'The Grim Reaper,' for his signature was on receipts for the human freight that he brought in — usually dead weight. Jesse James had a reputation of his own, as the West's most notorious outlaw. In 1882 in the Missouri township of St. Joseph the paths of the two men crossed. There could only be one outcome between the man who sought dollars and the man who sought survival — an unquestioned finality for one or the other . . .

B. J. HOLMES

DOLLARS FOR THE REAPER

Complete and Unabridged

LINFORD
Leicester

First published in Great Britain in 1990 by
Robert Hale Limited
London

First Linford Edition
published June 1992
by arrangement with
Robert Hale Limited
London

British Library CIP Data

Holmes, B. J.
    Dollars for the reaper.—Large print ed.—
Linford western library
I. Title II. Series
823.914 [F]

ISBN 0–7089–7180–6

F. A.

Printed and bound in Great Britain by
T. J. Press (Padstow) Ltd., Padstow, Cornwall

For Jo and Paul

For Jo and Paul

Foreword

The continuing absence of law along the western frontier of the United States during the latter half of the last century led to the phenomenon known to history as 'the bounty-hunter'. Unfortunately for students of the period, no systematic contemporary record was kept of the payment from public funds made to private citizens for delivery to the authorities of wanted persons. Therefore, as the evidence of their very existence is anecdotal, compounded by myth and legend, there can be no quantitative comparisons, no grisly league tables.

However, recent study of a particularly valuable cache of historical documents now lodged in the Archive Department of the Calpone Foundation Library has shown the name of one recipient of bounty payments to appear with noticeable regularity during the period. Nothing is known about him apart from his name, Jonathan Grimm, and that records show his fading signature on receipts for twenty-three men brought in dead or alive. With the data being incomplete, the actual figure that could be credited to him is likely to be even greater. Irrespective, the statistic as it stands must put him at, or near, the top of the league table of those men who earned their living by this questionable means.

The following text recounts an episode in that man's life. While there is no extant evidence as to its particulars, neither is there any to the contrary.

1

A ROAR of sound. It faded yet continued to echo like a thunderclap bouncing around the heavens of his mind. Then, weakening to a buzz. But still there.

He was confused and, in an attempt to make sense of his circumstances, he tried to grab at the strands of thought that swayed across his brain like submersed weeds in a stream. What had happened? But his mind and body were oddly, eerily separated. Where was he? Slowly he brought his powers of concentration to bear and he became vaguely aware that the buzzing resonance had been replaced by harsh cawing sounds. He began to feel heat on the back of his neck, pain in his forehead, and he hesitated to open his eyes, hoping to slip back into comfortable, painless drowsiness.

"You okay, mister?"

A voice, whose? He felt someone shaking him. He opened his eyes. His body and senses still seemed somewhat remote and he was surprised to find himself lying with his face pressed against soil. The gritty stuff was in his nose and coated his lips. He snuffled and tried to spit it out. He closed his eyes as someone rolled him over and shook him vigorously. Reluctantly he opened his eyes again but his head spun for some seconds before he could make out a face. Finally he managed to focus. He saw the face of a young man limned against the sun-filled sky. Beyond he caught sight of circling vultures.

"I asked if you was okay, mister?"

"Yeah," he grunted. The effort of speaking brought back his memory with a rush. Prairie. He'd been crossing open prairie. And the last thing he'd heard was the bony rattle of a sidewinder before his horse had reared.

2

"My horse?" he grunted. "How's my horse?"

"Don't worry yourself, mister. He's fine. I came across him some distance back. Reckon he was looking for water. I roped him, watered him and brung him with me. Then I came across you."

Jonathan Grimm tried to raise himself to take stock but couldn't. "Had a fall. Damned rattler spooked my horse."

"I figured something like that. Then I saw him or his mate working his way towards you. But don't worry. He ain't around no more. Blew his goddamn head off with one shot. Just in time. I don't reckon you been bit."

The explosion. A gunshot. That was it. The intrusive sound marking an action that had probably saved his life.

"No. I ain't bit. I'd sure know by now if I was. Judas Priest! I must have hit my head on a rock when I fell."

"Yeah. You got one helluva lump on the side of your head. And you've had

3

a touch of sun, too, by the look of you. I'll get you some water."

Grimm finally heaved himself up onto his elbow and shuddered at the sight of the headless, uncoiled serpent, now like a harmless length of slack rope, a few feet from where he was lying. He felt the lump on the side of his temple. His head was thumping; he was prone to headaches. His eyesight still hazy he glanced up and saw his horse munching at the grass. At least it was a relief to know his precious Andalusian was all right.

He watched the man go to his own horse and return with a canteen. He was of medium build with a shock of ginger hair. He took out the stopper and handed the canteen to the fallen man who gulped at the refreshing liquid. A minute later Grimm was standing groggily on his feet.

"By my reckoning," the man said, "there's a town some miles on. I'll see that you get there. We should make it in a couple of hours. We've seen the worst of the sun today."

"What town is that?"

"Jefferson Springs."

That made a bell ring loud and clear. It all came back. He had been heading for Jefferson Springs when he'd had the mishap. There'd been this bank clerk who'd absconded with funds and headed west. Name of Horatio Cary. The bank had put a small price on Mr Cary's head, an amount not enough to make it worth the while of an established bounty-hunter. However, the astute Mr Cary had taken a substantial amount of their liquid assets and, being a small local bank with uncovered deposits, it would have to close as a result of the theft — so for their own survival they had been forced to offer a considerable bonus, conditional on recovering a goodly portion of the missing finance. That made the reward big enough to attract the attention of a bounty-hunter of the stature of Jonathan Grimm.

"Name's Johnson," the young man said, putting out his hand. "Bob Johnson."

The bounty-hunter took it. "Jonathan Grimm." Then he chuckled drily. "I figure it goes without saying I'm mighty obliged to make your acquaintance."

"A fine piece of horse you got here," Johnson said as he tied a trailing-rope to the Andalusian's bridle. "Would have been a pity to lose him."

More than a pity, a helluva loss. It was a fine horse and had seen him through some scrapes. The younger man helped the elder into the saddle. Once mounted, Johnson gigged his own horse and they moved off.

They travelled in relative silence as Grimm recovered his grip on reality in the swaying saddle. About half an hour later they came to a complex of shacks with all the accoutrements of a stage relay station: a corral at the rear with replacement mules, a smithy with wheel rims hanging from the walls. But the visitors were more interested in the

6

well and trough. By the time they got there the stationman, having already spied them coming from a distance, was standing in the doorway under a crudely painted sign bearing the legend BLUE GRASS FLATS. He wore high-waisted pants with faded suspenders over a homespun shirt.

"Name's Luke," he said by way of greeting. He had a long horse face with an ever-open mouth, full of irregularly-shaped teeth. "What can I do for you guys?"

"Just passing through," Johnson explained. "Any charge for watering our hosses?"

"No, son. Help yourself. Glad of a bit of company if the truth were known. A stationman needs to be able to stand his own company when the only conversation he gets is with stage-drivers and shotguns — and that's just small-talk." He looked at Grimm who was not yet fully recovered. "You all right, mister?"

"Sure. All juice and vinegar." He

wasn't all 'juice and vinegar' but he didn't feel in the mood for talk.

"You don't look too frisky. Ain't run into any trouble I should know about?"

"Like what?" Grimm asked, lowering himself unsteadily out of the saddle.

"Injuns? Bushwhackers? Any infomation like that, I need to pass on to the stage-line."

Grimm walked over to the well while the younger man took charge of the horses. "No, nothing like that. Just had a fall, is all."

"That's good," the man said. Then added in an embarrassed tone, "I didn't mean that the way it might sound, mister. It's just that we ain't had no trouble around these parts for a long time."

The pulley-wheel above the well spun as Grimm lowered the bucket. Then he and Johnson used the dipper to drink and douse themselves with the cool, freshly drawn water.

"That's right," the stationman said

as they refreshed themselves. "You go ahead and take advantage while you can. The speed at which those railroad bozos are laying their tracks there ain't gonna be no stage-line soon. Hear tell in no time at all folks'll be able to drive on those fancy trains clear through to Cheyenne. This place'll fall derelict."

Grimm rested on the front porch and exchanged pleasantries with the man while his new companion watered the horses. "What will you do when they close this place?" he asked.

The stationman thumbed his suspenders. "Won't hit me. I'm coming up to retire-time anyways. Aim to settle in Jefferson Springs and spend my days in the saloons, getting all the conversation I been a-missing out on."

"How far is it to town?" Grimm asked.

"You should make it by nightfall."

"We better be moving on," the young man said, pulling the horses away from the trough. He knew enough not to let them drink too much.

They made their farewells and hit the trail once more.

2

INSIDE the judge's parlour, Sheriff Banner faced a sea of accusing eyes: the mayor, judge, lawyer and other businessmen and dignitaries of the town.

"We are very concerned about your behaviour," the judge said, his lined face and grey hair reinforcing the authority exuded by his tone of voice. "The circumstances of Biff's escape from custody are very questionable. And for you, with a full posse of eager and able citizens, to come up, empty-handed, displays incompetence on your part."

Banner nodded obsequiously.

"Everyone is equal under the law," the judge continued. "This is a very serious matter. For a law officer to show favouritism in the execution of his duty verges on corruption."

11

Banner stood submissively, arms down, working his cap rim nervously through his fingers. He'd never been able to hold a regular job in his life. His becoming sheriff (because no-one else wanted the job at the time) had led to the longest employment he'd ever had. And it wasn't the most arduous of jobs. He sure didn't want to lose it. He not only valued the salary, although it wasn't much more than that earned by a cowhand out on the range, but also the kickbacks he got regularly from half a dozen of the town big shots for turning a blind eye. He didn't ask any questions or check brands when cattle were moved into the slaughterhouse late at night. They were only small bunches and they didn't come from local herds. The real estate man was suspected of shady dealing on properties and Banner had gone through the motions but in reality had been deaf to complaints. And he kept the blue-stockings off the back of the madame who ran the cat-house. It was all harmless, but the greasing of his palm for these and other services more than doubled his take-home jack. If he lost the post, all that would go.

All because of his stupid cousin. He'd always said Biff was some cents short to the dollar in the brain department. The pattern was set when the kid was given that stupid name in the first place. Biff, what kind of a name was that to give anybody for Christ's sake?

Jefferson Springs didn't have much of a crime rate. A contretemps between drunks on a Saturday night made headline news. But of late there'd been some petty rustling locally. A cow or two here and there. Didn't amount to a hill of beans but Banner's cousin Biff had been suspected and Banner had resisted hints that he pursue the matter. Then the owner of a spread had caught him red-handed and brought him in. Banner had no option but to put him in the slammer pending trial. However, come morning the sheriff reported to the judge that his prisoner had escaped.

There was no explanation of how his cousin could have gotten through a locked iron-bar door — except for the redness in the face of the sheriff now standing before the town committee.

In the present circumstances cousin Biff's stupidity had been twofold. Stupid for operating within Banner's bailiwick and double-stupid for getting caught. Banner had no option but to let the moron go when no-one was looking. Banner lived with his mother and she was a strong-willed (not to mention strong-armed) woman who believed the world was divided into family and not-family. You didn't let kin down. She would have made life a living hell for Banner, maybe even have kicked him out of the house, if he hadn't left that jail door unlocked and gone for a walk.

Of course, he'd raised a posse for appearances' sake. But, having told Biff to make himself scarce by riding as far north as he could, the sheriff had taken his posse south, praying his dumb-cluck relative had a sense of direction.

After a day's riding around they'd come back empty-handed. It was then he'd been summoned to the judge's house where the town committee had been having a meeting. They were all squaredealers and no fools. Although they couldn't prove it, they knew Biff's escape had been the sheriffs doing.

"This is a very serious matter," the judge continued. "And you seem incapable of giving us a satisfactory explanation."

Banner looked sheepish. "Like I said, sir, maybe I forgot to lock the door in the heat of the moment. It can happen."

"Not to a sheriff it can't," the judge said cynically. "Not one that's worth his salt. It is our considered opinion that there was no forgetting about it." He paused. "However, do you like your job?"

"Yes, sir."

"And you want to hang onto it?"

"Yes, sir."

The judge glanced at his colleagues'

faces for endorsement and cleared his throat. "Well," he went on. "We have talked the matter over and, in the circumstances, have decided to give you a second chance. But mark my words, if you blot your copybook once more, we are going to have to put forward another candidate for the next election. It should be plain that a candidate supported by the committee would be likely to be elected. We want an active and effective law officer in Jefferson Springs."

"I understand, judge." Banner knew it would still be difficult to get someone willing to undertake the job but he also realized that if they put their mind to it they would be able to come up with someone. So it was a real threat.

The judge looked around again at his austere-looking colleagues. "Anything else, gentlemen?"

Their eyes conveyed their feeling that their spokesman had said it all and they shook their heads.

"Very well, Banner," the judge concluded. "You may go."

Thank you for your consideration, sir," the sheriff said and walked out onto the verandah. Outside, he pulled the faded Confederate cap firmly onto his head and set off back to his office, a scowl writ large on his features.

The man who called himself James Brown finished his dessert and pushed away the dish. "The best apple-pie I have ever tasted," he said. "My compliments, Mrs van Damm."

The lady was tidying up the table. "That's very kind of you to say so, Mr Brown," she said. "I like to see a man enjoying his food." She walked round to his side. "Hey, there's some left." She picked up the plate and slid the remaining portion into his dish with a serving-spoon. "There, you finish it off."

"I couldn't, thank you. I'm replete. Utterly satiated."

"Oh you and your big words," she

giggled. "You lawyers are all the same with your fancy way of talking."

"I'm not a lawyer, Mrs van Damm. I have told you before. I am a clerk, an assistant to a lawyer. There is a difference."

"Not much. Both occupations call for an educated man." She tapped his dish. "Anyway, replete or not, I insist. Now be a good boy."

She touched his neck, her fingers lingering. "You know, you raise the tone amongst the guests. Cowmen and penny-ante drummers, the rest of them. I've never had a lawyer staying before."

He declined to correct her again and busied himself with the pie as she left for the kitchen. He was all alone in the room, the other residents having gone about their business, leaving the table covered with plates, serving-dishes and eating-utensils. He finished off the pie, stacked the dish with others from the table and took the pile into the kitchen. "I'll give you a hand, Mrs van Damm."

"You shouldn't, you're a guest." Mrs

van Damm always called her boarders 'guests'. It was more refined.

"Now it's my turn to insist," he said and returned to the dining-room for another load. Minutes later, he was beside her, drying dishes.

"And what are your plans for this evening?" she asked.

"The usual. A little reading, I thought."

"Oh you and your books. You need to relax once in a while, you know."

"I find reading relaxing."

"You'll strain your eyes. Our eyes are very precious, you know. We should look after them. And you've got such beautiful eyes. Hazel, a lovely colour. But why must you hide them behind those horrible spectacles? And that beard! I do wish you'd shave it off. You have such a handsome face underneath, I'm sure." She clattered some washed cutlery on the draining-board. "Those go in the drawer." Then, "What do you read?"

"Novels mainly."

"What are you escaping from?"

He suddenly dropped the forks he was drying. "Escaping? What do you mean, Mrs van Damm?"

"Reading about the imagined adventures of imaginary people. That's escaping from the real world. What are you escaping from? An unhappy love-life perhaps?"

"Come, come, Mrs van Damm," he said, picking up the fallen cutlery and rinsing them in the water before drying them again. "I think you imbue the harmless act of reading with too much meaning."

They proceeded with their task in silence for a while. Then, "Is there a Mrs Brown?" she asked.

"Er, no. I never seemed to get around to marriage."

"Look, I have an idea," she said when she had nearly finished. "I'm having a little celebration tonight. Won't you join me?"

"A celebration? I wouldn't want to intrude on something private."

"You wouldn't be intruding. You see, now my husbands's gone I have no-one with whom to share these things and I do so dislike celebrating alone."

He coughed, finding it difficult to escape the corner he found himself being forced into. "What is the occasion?"

"Does one have to have an occasion?" She placed an upturned gravy-boat, the last washed item, on the draining-board. After he had dried it and put it on a shelf she took his hand very firmly and spoke softly. "You come to my room in half an hour. The wine will be ready and so will I." She giggled. "And by that time I will have thought of something to celebrate."

3

LIGHT was fading when Grimm and Johnson hit town. The bounty-hunter asked the young ginger-haired man if he could buy him a drink by way of thanks and the two men sat for a spell in a saloon. At the far end an old guy was tinkling on an upright piano and occasionally hitting the right notes. They established themselves as far from him as they could, grateful to slake their thirst and rest in relative peace and comfort. Their conversation held nothing of importance. Johnson was heading west to Colorado on family business while Grimm revealed nothing more than he was on the trail looking for work. It had been a long day and they were both tired and looking forward to sleep. Thanking Johnson for his help he quartered his horse at the livery stable and bedded down for the night on a pallet in a drovers' sleeping-house. He had the money for the best hotel in town — but there were times when his occupation required he kept a low profile. Hell, he was bushed.

Come dawn the next morning he strolled around the town reconnoitring the lay-out. It was no different from any other frontier town: a main street with one of everything to meet the needs of the meagre population of settlers and cowpunchers. He dropped into a chair under the verandah outside a general store and sat smoking his pipe, watching the rest of the town wake up.

There were those that saw the work of bounty-hunters as non-stop, action-packed adventure. But those people were dreamers with a myth they wished to believe in to counter their own humdrum lives. The reality behind the myth was that most of the bounty-hunter's time was taken up, when he wasn't wearing out his ass in the saddle, with merely using his eyes.

Observation was the key to pulling in the dollars — and to survival.

It had to be that way. For a start, a hunter's quarry would always be some guy who didn't want to be seen. That needed a keen eye, one that didn't miss much however insignificant. Then, when he had identified his man, he would perforce be moving into a situation that had the potential to be tight. It was a fact of life that most guys on the lam just didn't want to be caught. So, before moving into a face-up, you had to look at two things — your means of entrance into the situation — and your exit. Finally, a bounty-hunter always needed to keep his eyes on his back. The nature of his chosen profession involved the kind of work that made for vengeful enemies. Enemies with long memories.

And so, it was no chore for him to sit in that chair for most of the morning, for all the world like an unshaven, itinerant drover with time on his hands. Mid-morning he noted the ginger-haired Johnson leave his hotel, saddle up and head out of town. Then, before noon, he slowly did the round of the town's saloons; again watching and listening.

It was while he was taking hash in a cheap eats-house that, through the grimy window, he saw what might be his man. A small, slight figure crossing the street. Grimm quickly untied his bandanna, spat on it and used it to clear a view-hole through the glass. Yes, it was the man he was after. He was pretty sure. Despite the new and neatly tended beard, the fellow was recognizable to a man whose livelihood depended on seeing through varied attempts at disguise. The man wore a derby but under the hat Grimm knew he had a prematurely receding hairline. He chuckled as he watched the man falter and fumble with his feet at the boardwalk. The poor fellow was deliberately not wearing the glasses he needed for short-sightedness and was staggering around town as a consequence.

Grimm made to rise as he watched the man mount the boardwalk. Goddamn pity. Although he was starving, he would have to leave half his meal to keep track of the fellow. Then he saw the man enter the lawyer's office. He seemed familiar with the place and didn't knock. Either he was a client or he worked there. There had been nothing furtive about the man's manner so Grimm reckoned he had time to finish off his meal after all. He did so keeping his eye on the unopened door across the thoroughfare.

When he'd finished he left the eats-house and crossed the street. Directly outside the lawyer's office he leant against the awning support and lit up his pipe while he read the sign elegantly etched on the frosted glass: JOSIAH EATON, ATTORNEY-AT-LAW. After a few minutes a little old lady bustled past him, knocked on the door and entered. Between the opening and closing of the door he caught a glimpse of Cary, now wearing his glasses and with a green eyeshade over his thinning hair, at a reception desk. That was it. He'd got himself a job as a clerk in the lawyer's office. There would be an easy transfer of skills from bank-clerking to tending to a lawyer's paperwork. And being able to read and write in a useable degree was at such a premium out west that an employer in need would only be too grateful to take on someone without checking too deeply into his background.

Now certain of his man and his whereabouts, Grimm crossed the street and went through the door labelled Sheriff Banner. Another rule of his trade was the advisability of clearing with the local law before acting whenever possible. Most law officers didn't cotton to bounty-hunters. They were envious of the money they could pull and the way that they could operate without being hamstrung by ordinances and regulations. Even without prejudice, officers could foul up a face-up by interfering when weapons were pulled just because they didn't know the set-up and who was on what team. So, by notifying them beforehand, at least you got things straight. Being treated with a little dignity was all that many of them wanted.

"Where's the sheriff? Grimm asked.

The reason he put the question, the man seated before him didn't look like a sheriff. He had straight, clean-cut features, long fine hair and a beard. He had more the look of conventional paintings of the Messiah — except for the faded Confederate peaked cap. In fact, on the surface he had some of the same qualities of the religious figure: genial, unassuming. But those who knew him were aware of a disposition that could lead to a harsh temper if things didn't go his way.

"I'm the sheriff," he said quietly with some sort of smile in the blue eyes. "Sheriff Banner at your service, sir."

"To start with, sheriff, some information, if you please. You know the young man working over at the lawyer's office? Short feller, beard."

"You mean working for Josiah Eaton?"

"Yeah, that's him."

"Don't *know* him, not as such. But I seen him about."

"What does he call himself?"

"Brown, if I recall rightly."

"He's a stranger in town, ain't he?"

"Yeah."

"How long's he been working there?"

The lawman sucked in breath while he thought. "Couple of weeks." Then he straightened up in his seat and his demeanour changed. He had enough on his plate without being probed by a stranger. "Say, mister. why all these questions?"

He looked more attentively at his visitor's face and noticed a scatteration of black marks, high on his cheekbone near his eye. A long-ingrained powderburn. "Anyways, who are you?"

29

"I'll come to the point, sheriff. My name is Grimm. Jonathan Grimm." He took out his poster of Cary, unfolded it and laid it before the lawman. "That's your Mister Brown. Real name: Horatio Cary."

Disbelief registered on Banner's face. "An owlhooter? That pipsqueak?" He looked at the crumpled wanted-sheet. It was a fuzzy reproduction of some domestic studio portrait that must have been found in Cary's belongings after he'd vamoosed. He was bareheaded, with a high collar, and a tall opera hat held stiffly against his chest. It must have been several years old. "And that don't look too much like him neither."

Grimm gave an impatient grunt. "You've been in the business long enough to know dodgers ain't never precise replicas. But that's him all right. Horatio Cary. One-time bank clerk. Wanted in Kansas for taking off with funds. There's a price on his head. That makes him open game and I'm here to notify you that I am taking him into custody in a private capacity."

Banner looked up at the tall gaunt man looming over his desk. "A bounty, eh?"

"That's what some folks call me, sheriff." There was no more point to the conversation so he turned and opened the door. "If you're interested in running a check you can wire the Law Office at Kansas City. They'll give you whatever confirmation you want. Either way, I'm attending to the matter right now."

Leaving the sheriff not too sure what to do next, he exited and strode down the boardwalk.

4

GETTING to the lawyer's office Grimm opened the door. Cary looked up as the bounty-hunter made his appearance. Now without his derby, the little man looked a mite more like his poster. "Yes, sir?"

"I'd like to see Mr Eaton."

"I'm afraid he only sees clients by appointment, sir."

"I ain't no client, son," Grimm said. "I got something he should know about." Then, adding "Mr Eaton!" loudly, he moved beyond the clerk and opened a second door. An elderly man was at a desk working on a document. "Mr Eaton," Grimm said before the surprised man could say anything, "I have some information for you." Then, leaving the door open, he moved back to Cary and stood at his side in order to block him if he chose to run.

"You're going to have to find yourself a new clerk," the hunter went on as the old man came into the reception room spluttering, "What is the meaning of this?"

Grimm dropped the opened poster on the desk by way of explanation. He looked past Cary. "This man means U.S. scrip to me. Real name's Horatio Cary and I'm taking him in." He gripped his quarry's shoulder and pulled him firmly to his feet. "You can come without a fuss, or otherwise. It's a free country — the choice is yours."

"I don't know what you mean," Cary spluttered. "Where are you taking me?"

"You're wanted in Kansas. You know it, I know it. That's all we need to get the show on the road."

"Is this true, James?" Eaton asked, his voice reflecting wounded dignity.

Cary thought about it for a second then shrugged as best he could within the iron grip. "Yes, sir. My name isn't James Brown. It's Horatio Cary." A mouse of a man, he wouldn't have known how to resist even if he'd wanted to. "I wondered how long it would be," he said in a lowered voice.

"You can get your belongings," Grimm grunted. "You got a horse?"

"Er, no."

"No matter. That can be arranged."

"I'm not skilled in horse-riding."

"Huh, the distance we got to cover, you'll learn."

"I don't understand all this," Eaton put in, trying to inject some authority into his voice.

"That ain't my concern, mister," Grimm said. "See Sheriff Banner." With that he hauled his prisoner out into the sunlight. "What kind of place you staying at?"

"I have lodgings at Mrs van Damm's boarding-house, sir."

Grimm was partial to the 'sir'. He'd been called a lotta names by the coyotes he'd taken in but 'sir' was a new one. "While we're going over there I can handcuff you or walk alongside you with my gun in your ribs. What'll it be?"

"Oh dear, Mrs van Damm wouldn't take kindly to either."

"Well, if those two options embarrass you there is a third. It's a long haul to Kansas City and you and me have got a lotta trail to get behind us. So, in the interests of goodwill, I could start by giving you one chance to let me trust you. As a trial, you give me your word not to cause any trouble and we won't use the cuffs or the gun. But don't abuse it."

Cary took off his glasses and cleaned them, then used the handkerchief to wipe his sweating forehead. "I won't be any trouble, Mr Grimm."

"Lead the way, Horatio."

Outside, Grimm looked at the sun. It was still afternoon and, it was true, they could get in some hours' travel, but the Andalusian was bushed. It would be better to head out in the morning with fresh horses. The two men continued to the boarding-house.

A genteel lady, Mrs van Damm looked askance at the tall, dusty stranger intruding with his dirty boots into her clean house. Not the sort of fellow she would have expected the respectable Mr Brown to associate with at all.

"I'm staying over the night in Mr Brown's room, Grimm said. Now he had decided to leave in the morning they had an overnight stay and there was more privacy here than at the drovers' lodge. "That okay with you, ma'am?" As he walked he tripped over some rugs she had scattered over the floor. Used to bare wooden planking he had trouble negotiating such refinements, especially in riding-boots.

"What is this all about, James?" she asked.

Cary was nonplussed and didn't speak.

"I'm a business associate," Grimm put in. "Kind of."

Mrs van Damm looked Grimm up

and down again. "What kind of business?" she asked suspiciously.

"My name's Grimm, ma'am. Jonathan Grimm." The tone of his voice displayed an attempt to recapture some dignity after his ungainly stumbling. "I supply a service for the authorities."

"Businessman or not, I only take gentlefolk," she said coldly.

The bounty-hunter was getting impatient. "I am gentlefolk," he said, a sudden firmness coming to his voice as he moved his jacket to reveal his guns.

"In that case, I suppose it's all right," she said with trepidation but no conviction. "If it's all right with James. But mind those spurs on the woodwork and upholstery."

He followed his prisoner upstairs to the accompaniment of loud tutting from below. Inside Cary's bedroom Grimm looked the place over. A vase of flowers was on a bedside table. Somebody got the treatment. And either the landlady had just changed the sheets or the bed hadn't been slept in. He shrugged and unclipped the handcuffs from his belt. "I can't trust you all the time," he said, using them to fix one of Cary's wrists to the brass bedstead. He returned downstairs where Mrs van Damm kept a silent but critical surveillance as he crossed the parlour and went outside. He collected his own gear from the drovers' doss-house, then made his way to the ostler's, finding him working the bellows on a fire in preparation for some horse-shoeing. Grimm ensured his own horse was well fed and bedded on dry straw, then checked that there was another horse and saddle he could buy for Cary. He dickered over the price for a spell, stepping outside when a satisfactory arrangement had been made.

"Oh, James!" Mrs van Damm said, her hand shooting to her mouth. She'd gone up to his bedroom when she'd seen the dirty stranger leave the house.

Ashamed, Cary turned his head away from her. She sat on the bed beside him. "What's going on?"

"You'll have to stop calling me James," he said, his face still to the wall. "My name's Horatio. Horatio Cary. And I've done something bad."

"Bad? Bad?" She gripped his arm as she spoke. "You couldn't do something bad. You're too gentle a man."

"I am a bank-robber, Marjorie."

"No."

"You'll have to face it, it's true. And I've lied to you about my name."

"This is some kind of weird game, James. I know you well enough to know you couldn't walk into a bank with a gun! Don't be silly!"

"I didn't do it like that. I took it from my employer when I worked in a bank. It's called embezzlement. That's why I grew the beard you don't like and came to Jefferson Springs. To hide myself away under a different name.

"And who's that horrible man?"

"He's what they call a bounty-hunter.

There's a reward for me and he's after it."

She plunged her face into her hands and he could hear her crying. "I'm sorry, Marjorie. I've deceived you."

"Oh, I had such hopes for us," she said into her fingers.

He turned, the shame on his face transforming to puzzlement. "High hopes? I don't understand, Marjorie."

"Yes. I was dearly hoping that we might get closer. In fact I was hoping that we might . . . get married."

"Married? I am a bank clerk, Marjorie. At least I was. I couldn't have supported you. Not in the manner of your life as I've seen it. A bank teller can't afford wine, fancy food and expensive clothes for his wife."

"Oh, James. That's unimportant."

"What do you mean?"

She composed herself somewhat. "There was no mortgage on the boarding-house. When William died he left it to me. It doesn't make a fortune but it brings in a good living. Enough to buy the things you mentioned. Enough for two, if needs be."

"I didn't know that was in your thoughts when we . . . "

"Of course it was. I wouldn't go to bed with anybody. You're the only one since William passed away. Oh James, I loved you." She ran her fingers over the cold, hard metal of the handcuffs. "I still do." She composed herself a little further. "This is too much to take in one go." She sniffed while she reflected. "Will you go to prison?"

"Yes. I'm guilty. That's a fact. No disputing."

"Oh." Then, "How long will you get?"

"I don't know. These matters are all new to me."

Resolution permeated her face. "It doesn't matter. I'll wait."

Grimm stopped in his tracks on his return journey to the hotel. A trail-dusty rider had just dismounted opposite and was fixing his horse to a hitch-rail. He never forgot a face.

Especially when they were associated with a pair of tied-down side pistols. It was Lee Hammersley — a rival in Grimm's trade — dressed wholly in black[1]. The man saw his occupation as a profession on a par with that of a doctor or a lawyer and he dressed as he thought accordingly. Grimm knew Hammersley well enough to know the guns in place on his hips meant he was close to his quarry. As a professional he didn't carry the tools of his trade all the time. A surgeon didn't keep his scalpel permanently at the ready; it was out of sight and only taken out when he needed it. It was the same with Hammersley's black, well-oiled Smith & Wessons.

They were in place now, so who was he after? Cary? Or someone else? Grimm didn't know of anybody else

---

[1] Some of Lee Hammersley's earlier history is recorded in 'HAZARD' published by Robert Hale.

in Jefferson Springs that was worth a bounty-hunter's time. It must be Cary he was closing in on. Grimm was not unduly perturbed. Hammersley was fast but in a face-up Grimm could handle him. Ahead, however, lay at least a week's cross-country trek with his prisoner.

He turned his back lest he himself be recognized. No point in looking for trouble. He continued to keep a check on Hammersley's movements via the reflection in a store window.

Slight change of plan. He waited until the man had disappeared into a saloon and then made his way to the stage despatch office where he booked passage for two to Junction City. There were several folks in the room. That was good. The more it got around he and his prisoner were on the stage the better. Then he returned to the livery stable.

The ostler was at a critical stage in shoeing a horse and Grimm knew better than to interrupt. He watched as the man burned an iron into the hoof held firmly between his legs and hammered in the nails.

"Got another proposition," he said as the ostler clenched off the nail-ends.

The man lowered the hoof to the ground and stepped back to watch how the horse stood on its new footwear. "Yeah?" he said, wiping his hands on the leather apron around his waist.

"I don't want nobody to see me leave town on horseback. There's two of us catching the morning stage for Junction City. Before the stage leaves I would like you to take the saddled horses outta town."

"Go on."

"You know the relay station at Blue Grass Flats?"

"Sure."

"I would want you to stay there with the horses and make the transfer when we come through."

"That could be arranged. What's in it for me? As you can see, I'm a busy man."

"Forget the financial arrangement we've already made. I'll give you your original asking-price for the horse and saddle. On top I'll throw in twenty bucks for your time — and for keeping your mouth shut."

The ostler nodded appreciatively. "It's a deal, mister. You got your own reasons and I don't wanna know 'em. You can rely on me, pal. What time do you want me to leave?"

5

IT was just after dawn that the stage started loading up, light enough for some folks to be going about their business. Grimm deliberately hung about on the boardwalk with his prisoner as the vehicle was being prepared and, as he guessed and hoped, passers-by showed more than a little interest in the pair of handcuffed figures. The more people who saw them leaving by stagecoach the better. When the stage finally pulled out, Grimm noted with satisfaction the curious eyes along the boardwalk and he settled back against the padded rest, content in the knowledge that the story of his departure with Cary by stage would soon get around town.

Mrs van Damm stood in the front room of her boarding-house, peering from behind a drape. Tearfully she'd made her goodbyes and had watched with chagrin as the cold-hearted bounty-hunter had handcuffed the man she'd come to love. She'd told her man to keep in touch and she would be waiting when he came out. From her window she'd seen them board the stage, then she'd watched it start to roll and disappear from her limited view. Now she returned to her room to cry it out of her system. Her remaining boarders would be getting no breakfast this morning.

Once the stage was bouncing along the trail Grimm unlocked the chain connecting him to Cary. Besides them there were four other passengers a woman and three men. All ordinary, law-abiding-looking folk. Directly opposite Grimm sat a middle-aged man in a three-piece suit with his head buried in a newspaper. As they rocked with the rhythm of the coach, Grimm studied him for want of something to do to pass the time. Eyebrows arched inwards, mouth turned down at the edges, worry was clearly a permanent expression on the poor guy's face. Grimm mused on what kind of life a fellow like that led. Maybe it was reading newspapers that got him down. Eventually the fellow laid aside his paper but his face didn't alter.

"May I?" Grimm asked, indicating the paper. A bounty-hunter kept his eyes and ears open all the time. And that included keeping up to date through newspapers when he had the chance.

"Sure. Go ahead," the unhappy-looking man said. "But you'll find it's all bad news."

No, it wasn't. First thing Grimm saw when he opened it was a piece on Jesse James. They hadn't caught him yet. Or his brother Frank. That was good news. Meant there was still a chance for the Grim Reaper. Now, there was an opportunity. What did the reward for Jesse stand at now? He scrutinized the text. Ten thousand smackeroos.

He might even think of retiring if he pulled in a haul like that. Not that he hadn't tried. It was back in '76 that he'd been close behind Cole Younger. Just a matter of the right circumstances and he'd have got him. Huh, then the goddamned peace officers set up a trap at Northfield.

He remembered it well. A black day for bounty-hunters. A lot of lucrative targets disappeared from the list. The James and Younger gang had planned to rob the bank at Northfield but what they didn't know was that the law would be waiting. All the big fish got trapped. Many were just mown down in the ambush: Bill Chadwell, Cleland Miller, Charlie Pitts. Those that surrendered were all now lifers in the slammer — amongst them the four Younger brothers: John, Cole, Jim and Bob.

Huh, John Younger had been the miracle. Had eleven bullets in him when he finally gave up. How does a guy live through a hail of bullets like that? Well, he'd survived. You live and learn.

Grimm smiled to himself when he remembered the fate of some of them. Poor old Miller had been shot down by a bystander who happened to be a medical student. The guy asked the federals for permission to keep the body which he'd then rendered down to a skeleton as an aid to his studies! And the last thing he'd heard was that Charlie Pitts had been mummified and was earning cents for some entrepreneur in a sideshow.

All of them gone or doing time.

Except Frank and Jesse. That would be a coup. Jesse James, hiding away somewhere, just waiting to be took. But there were no clues. He hadn't been seen or heard of since last year. There had been the Chicago and Rock Island train knockover at Winston, when they'd shot a passenger. It had been the murder that had jacked up the price on him. Then his last known caper: the Chicago and Alton Railroad at Glendale, Missouri.

And most of the loot from years of bank and railroad robbing hadn't been recovered. In one take — the Missouri-Pacific express which they knocked over at Ottersville, Missouri back in '76 — they'd heisted over a hundred thousand smackeroos! The biggest haul ever, anyplace. Some of that was still about. The Pinkertons were still active on the case. But if they couldn't crack it, with all their resources . . .

Jonathan Grimm was musing on the picture of Jesse and thinking "One day, my beauty . . . " when the lady passenger sighted the relay station. Grimm closed the paper, returned it to its owner and looked at his watch. With a team of fresh mules up front it had taken much less than the last time he'd made the journey, slumped in the saddle on a tired horse behind Bob Johnson.

With a "Whoa" from the driver they pulled in. "Won't be long, folks," he shouted to the passengers. "Just stopping to pick up any mail that might have come in from settlers."

With an "Excuse me, ma'am" to the woman, Grimm pushed open the door and pulled Cary with him. Time to let the driver know his load was going to he lightened. As he got down he saw the ostler waiting. All going to plan. He made his explanations to the driver as old Luke passed up a bag of mail.

"Whatever you say, sir," the driver said to Grimm. "But I ain't empowered to give no refund, you understand."

Grimm shook his head dismissively; a refund was the last thing that was on his mind at the moment.

"Some reading-matter, Luke," the driver said, handing down a parcel. "Magazines and such. Afraid the newspapers will be a mite outta date."

"You know that don't bother me," the stationman said. "Thanks."

There was a "Hap, hap!" from the driver and the four standing men watched the stage roll on towards the east in a cloud of dust. Grimm turned to the ostler and paid him the balance on their deal. The man told him how it was a pleasure doing business with him, mounted his own horse and headed back to town. Grimm turned to the stationman and slipped him a couple of double eagles. "Anybody comes a-calling," he said with a wink, "you ain't seen us leave the stage. As far as you know, we're headed for Junction City with the rest of them."

"Ain't that a fact," the stationman grinned, pocketing, the coins. "Shucks, I ain't seen nobody get off no place."

Grimm stroked the muzzle of his own horse then checked the saddles of the two. When he'd finished he tied a lead rope from his saddle-horn to the second.

"I've told you, mister," Cary said, apprehension writ big in his eyes, "I don't know much about horses."

"Just get your ass in the saddle and leave the rest to the animal."

When they were mounted, Grimm

eyed the stage, now a dark speck writing its signature in dust in the distance. Then he looked north and south. Not much to choose. It was a matter of making a commitment then seeing how the terrain shaped up. With an "Adios" to the stationman he gigged his horse northward, with the intent of curving east at an appropriate juncture.

Despite the noise made by the varied bummers and drovers as they rose, Lee Hammersley had had a hard day in the saddle and so was late getting out of his bunk this morning. After dousing his head under the hand-pump in back, he squared up to a platter of beans and eggs in the eats-house. On that he could ride all day — if his horse could take it. He'd been after this penpushing guy who'd vamoosed with a small fortune from a bank in Kansas. The trail had gone cold but he'd put in several weeks already and wasn't giving up now. Like all bounty-hunters he had his own grapevine — a network of contacts that supplied him with information for a fee — newspapermen, law officers, saloon bums — and he knew the runt he was after was moving west.

He came out of the eats-house and stood in the midmorning sun scratching his stubbled chin as he looked up and down the street. He belched and came to a decision. One drink, a few questions, and if nothing was forthcoming he'd head out following the sun.

Minutes later he was leaning on a saloon bar, foot on the rest. Close, sitting at a table, there was a bunch of unemployed saddle-bums to whom he paid little attention as they jawboned their time away.

"I didn't see him," one was saying.

"That's because you don't get up in a morning," another chided. "I bet you never caught no early worms!" The speaker lit a cigarette and kept his clenched fist hard against his mouth while he drew deep. "Mean-looking hombre, he was." Smoke came from his mouth as he spoke. "Tall and wiry. Got the little guy chained to him."

Hammersley was still only half listening, concentrating more on the whiskey that was putting some much needed life into his gut. That is until he heard the man say, "The scuttlebutt is that the feller's a bounty-hunter. Ain't proper law at all."

The bounty-hunter's ears pricked up. Somebody was escorting a prisoner: his line of country. "Excuse me prodding in, pardner. What was that you were saying?"

The drinker looked across, made some assessment of his questioner, then described what he had seen. Hammersley took Cary's dodger from his waistcoat pocket and placed it on the beer-damp table. "This little guy you're talking about — he look anything like this?"

The speaker took stock of it with his comrades looking over. "Could be, mister. You must have only just ridden into Jefferson Springs otherwise you would have heard som'at. It's been the talk of the town since yesterday. This bounty-hunter hombre picked him up from old Josiah Eaton's law office. The little tyke had been pen-pushing there for weeks. Nobody'ud a-guessed he was a wanted man. Didn't look the type. Scrawny little feller. Jeez, you never can tell."

"The one who collected him, the other fellow — tall and wiry, you say?"

"Yeah."

"And what did he look like? His face, for instance?"

The man at the table pondered. "Old and wrinkled. Pale, like his skin had never see'd the sun."

"Black powder-burns?" Hammersley prompted, touching his cheekbone with his fingers.

"Yeah. That's him."

The Reaper! Jonathan Grimm. Couldn't be anyone else! Not with the face of a well-kept grave. And the bastard had got the man he'd been after! That was enough for Hammersley. "Which way's the stage headed?"

"East."

Hammersley nodded a "Thanks", dropped some coins on the table with a "Have a drink, pardner" and headed for the batwings.

The leader of the conversation studied the coins then looked at the departing man. "I'll tell you better'n that, pardner" he shouted, revelling in feeling part of the action. "If you wanna know where they're headed — the bounty-hunter booked tickets for Junction City."

6

GRIMM was munching on a piece of hardtack but his prisoner was not interested in eating. The bounty-hunter had reined in to give the horses a rest and get them out of the high sun for a spell. He'd picked a spot beyond the top of a broken swell, so that he could get a distant view of their back-trail without showing himself against the sky.

"We'll get spare horses first chance," he said, more to himself than his companion. You don't make lengthy treks with single horses; he'd thought of that. But he'd also reasoned it would have been too cumbersome for the ostler to take out four horses to the relay station. And it would have increased the chance of the man being seen and questions being asked back in town. He took a drink from his canteen and, as he did so, looked at Cary leaning against the hole of a cottonwood. He sure didn't look like a criminal.

"Where did you hide the money you took?" he asked.

Cary remained silent.

"They're gonna ask you that when I hand you over," Grimm pressed. "Sooner or later you're gonna have to tell. May as well tell me now."

"You know, Mr Grimm," Cary said. "I been thinking. I figure your payment for taking me in, at least in part, will be conditional on the money being recovered."

Grimm didn't respond. It was the first time Cary had spoken for a long time. If he's gonna speak, the bounty-hunter thought, let him carry on.

There was a pause, then the little man continued. "So I'm saying nothing. That way, I ain't worth much to you. So you might as well let me go."

Grimm took another swig, stoppered his canteen, and kept his silence.

"You don't know," Cary went on, "I might have spent it."

Grimm looked at the beat-up derby and the threadbare suit. "I can't see no sign about your person of you having spent thousands of dollars!"

"But the point is — you don't know. I might have given it away to some worthy cause — or lost it. Whatever the reason, you're going to have to get used to the notion that I'm not the asset you thought I was."

Grimm stood up, walked down to where the horses where grazing and took the reins. "Come on, Cary. Mount up."

Josiah Eaton sat at his desk. He had documents to work up and no clerical help. His right hand was in a permanent fist and he worked the fingers of the hand, constantly bending his thumb against it. A sure sign of frustration, as his wife well knew.

Jehosophat! Another chore to do. There was that money in the safe in escrow — it all needed recording. God, he'd have to do it himself until he could get another assistant. He stood up, circled his desk and went to the safe. He twisted the knob this way and that in line with the combination, slung open the heavy door and took out the stacked metal boxes. He opened them up and stacked the money on his desk. He took some paper from a drawer and jotted down amounts as he counted them.

He got to the end. That was odd. He knew there should be about five hundred dollars more than he could tally. Maybe he'd made a mistake. He wasn't very good at mundane tasks — that's why he employed others, for God's sake. He re-stacked the bills and counted again. No, the sum was short of five hundred dollars, he was sure. He went back to the safe and explored the interior. No more cash. Where the hell was it? Sometimes his missus helped herself to petty cash when she needed some small item for the house and he wasn't about. But that was only cents out of a trouser pocket. And she didn't know the combination to the safe anyway.

He stood up while he thought about it. Then he felt sick. That Brown fellow — or Cary — or whatever he was called. He was a bank-robber, wasn't he? Jeez, the bastard had been helping himself to my funds too!

"I'm telling you, sheriff, the roulette wheel in that damn place is fixed." The salesman in Sheriff Banner's office was a bumptious, balding man with a sweat-stained suit stretched over his pudgy body. Whatever commission he got from selling his insurance policies went on wenching and gambling in the towns on his route. "And there's a lot of dealing off the bottom of the deck. I know about these things, sheriff. And I've told you how they do it."

Sheriff Banner nodded in a fake-understanding way. "What you aiming to do now, sir?" he asked, feigning interest.

"Well I have to move on to the next town. But I felt I just had to put in an official complaint before I left. It's scandalous."

"Quite right for you to do so, too," Banner said. "We can't have this sort of thing going on in our town." He fingered the piece of paper in front of him. "I have made a note. You can be on your way, resting assured that I will investigate."

"He'll be prosecuted, won't he?"

"Justice will be done."

"Much obliged, sheriff."

"And thank you for reporting the matter," the lawman said, opening the door obsequiously. "Law and order depends a lot on good citizens like yourself acting in this way."

As the man left, Josiah Eaton squeezed past him to enter.

"What can I do for you, Mr Eaton?" Banner said, balling the piece of paper and throwing it into his waste-bin,

64

making a mental note that he must tell the casino-owner not to be quite so blatant in his scamming of visitors.

"I been robbed, sheriff."

"Robbed? Who by?"

"That deceitful bastard who I have had the goodness of heart to have in my employ these last months. Brown, or Cary, whatever his goddamned name is. There's five hundred dollars missing from my safe."

"You sure it's him that's took it?"

"Has to be. It was in the safe and he and I are the only ones who know the combination. Huh, to think how I trusted him — and him a bank-robber!"

"He went out on the stage, didn't he?" Banner mused. "Chained to that bounty-hunter?"

"Yes."

Banner felt a surge through his body. Eaton was one of the squaredealers on the committee. This was the sheriffs chance to redress his standing with the town council and thereby secure his reappointment. "Don't worry, Mr Eaton. It's just a matter of catching up with the stage. That'll be no problem on horseback. We'll soon get the varmint and your money. Easy pie."

A rider stopped his horse. "Quick, Arch," he said, wheeling his mount towards a thicket. "Pull into cover. Horses ahead."

His companion followed suit. "I didn't see none."

"You will. They've just been obscured by that upthrust." He pointed. "A whole passel of 'em. Don't look wholesome."

"Yeah, I see 'em now, Dick." The large group was on the regular trail, moving in their direction. They wouldn't have passed close however because Arch Clements and Dick Liddell didn't ride regular trails themselves unless they had to.

The one called Liddell counted aloud as the figures became clearer. "Seven.

And eating trail at a lick. Reckon that's a posse, Arch."

"Yeah, that's my figuring too. Huh, I seen welcomer sights." They waited until the riders were well to their rear before pulling out and continuing. They were tired and didn't speak. Some time later they passed through a saddle lying between two ridges which enabled them to see far into the distance. A cluster of buildings was visible. Dick shielded his eyes as they neared. "A stage relay station," he said. "We'll see what it has to offer. And we might be able to get some information."

At Blue Grass Flats, old Luke was sitting on the verandah reading one of the magazines left by the stage, and looked up to see the two riders approaching. "Mighty busy today," he said to himself.

He flicked over some more pages while he waited for them to get close.

"We passed a bunch a short spell back," Liddell said after the howdies were over. "Fair humming along the trail. Passed us by without a by-your-leave. That be a posse?"

"Sure thing," Luke said, putting down his magazine. "That'd be Sheriff Banner out of Jefferson Springs."

"They must be after somebody?"

"Sure are."

"We figured so. Any ideas who they were after?"

"Stage had got a bounty-hunter aboard, taking some trash to justice back east." He still honoured his agreement with Grimm and didn't disclose the change to horseback.

"You know the renegade's name?"

"No."

Liddell nodded without interest and looked west. "According to my reckoning, next town's Jefferson Springs. That so?"

"Yeah. Just keep to the trail."

The riders dismounted. "How far?" Liddell asked of the stationman.

"Take you a couple of hours or more, seeing's your horses are tuckered. You're mighty welcome to water."

While Clements tended to the watering of the horses Liddell looked away and stared down the trail again for a minute. "You heard of a guy called Cary? He'd be new to these parts."

"Probably wouldn't be using his real name," Clements added. "Might have got work in a bank or something if he ain't lying low."

"You're making your enquiries of the wrong man, young'un," Luke grunted with a chuckle. "I don't get to town much and so don't get much of the scuttlebutt."

"Short fellow. Black hair. Usually wears glasses."

Luke smiled. "No offence, but ain't no point in giving me descriptions. I don't see folk. The only short bozo I seed for months was chained to a bounty-hunter this morning."

Liddell looked at Clements.

"How did you know he was short," he went on, "if he was in the stage?"

Luke suddenly wished he hadn't said anything but responded quickly. "They got out to stretch their legs during the stop-over."

"This guy," Clements put in. "The prisoner. He look anything like a bank teller?"

"No. He wasn't no bank teller. I know that much. Heard something about him working in Josiah Eaton's law office. Leastways, till the bounty put the cuffs on him! Huh!"

"Then why was the posse after him if he was already in the charge of the bounty?"

"Seems like he'd been helping himself to the cash in Josiah's safe!"

Seconds later, old Luke was standing in a swirl of slowly settling dust watching the two riders head back east, hot after the stage. "Now what the hell has fired them up?" His joints creaked as he moved back to his chair on the verandah and settled down with his magazine.

7

EVENTUALLY the posse was within sight of the bouncing stage. Sheriff Banner was glad. He needed something to put him back in the good books of the town council. Election time was near and, Jefferson Springs being such a quiet town where not much happened, a job like this with some glamour and efficiently concluded would show he could handle the business. It would certainly put him on the good side of Josiah Eaton; him being on the town council — for starters that couldn't be bad.

As the riders neared he pointed for one of his men to spur forward and undertake the task of stopping the vehicle. When the lead rider caught up, he flailed his arm back and forth to flag down the vehicle.

"Sheriffs posse out of Jefferson Springs," he yelled above the clatter of wheel rims and creaking thoroughbraces.

The driver threw a sideways glance and saw Banner thumbing his badge. "Whoa," he shouted, pulling hard on the ribbons and hitting the brake.

Sheriff Banner reined in and blinked through the dust. "We're relieving you of one of your occupants!"

"At this rate," the driver muttered to his shotgun, "we're gonna ride into Junction City with an empty stage."

"Wanted for theft back in town," the sheriff explained.

The driver looked quizzical. "What the hell are you talking about? Who, for God's sake?" He shrugged when he saw the no-nonsense look Banner was giving him. "Oh well, help yourself, sheriff. But they all look law-abiding to me."

"Law-abiding?" the sheriff queried, leaning from the saddle in an attempt to look through the window into the interior. "This one's chained to a bounty-hunter. That don't exactly give the appearance of being law-abiding, does it? Ha!"

"Oh, him," the driver said. "Why didn't you say? The pair of 'em changed to horses at the relay station. Way back at Blue Grass Flats."

Banner snorted as he confirmed for himself that the man he sought was not there. "Tarnation!" he snapped. He took off his dusty Confederate cap and wiped his brow. "Which way they head from the station?"

The driver shrugged. "Wished I could help, sheriff, but I didn't see." He leant over the side. "Any of you folk tell the way they went?" he enquired of the passengers. Nobody had.

The anger of frustration clouded Banner's eyes as he slammed his hat back on his head and pointed for his men to return whence they had come.

The evening sun was close to the horizon and stretched long shadows over the trail as the Reaper and his prisoner approached the small township of Knox Creek. The only feature of distinction at the perimeter was the notice which was just legible in the fading light to the effect that a town ordinance forbade the discharge of firearms beyond that point. They passed the shacks which fringed the town's outermost section and made their way to the large structure which had to be a livery stable. Outside, Grimm dismounted and watched Cary lower himself stiffly to the ground. The man looked tired and a little older. "Shucks, I told you I wasn't used to horses," he said, collapsing against the hitch-rail.

Grimm tied the reins to the rail. "A sore butt never hurt nobody. Before you get to Kansas City you're gonna be riding like you was born in the saddle." He said the words for effect but knew they weren't true. Some folks — and this Cary bum was one of them — would never learn. For some time now the Reaper had been cursing inwardly at their slow progress. Even though the man had nothing to do but sit tight and be trailed as a passive appendage, the arrangement had been a drag on their pace. Still, he consoled himself, there was no rush.

After he had lodged the horses and taken a meal he booked in at the town's only hotel.

As the two riders emerged through the throat of the low pass they saw a group of riders approaching them up the slope.

"Jeez!" Clements hissed, instinctively whipping his horse to the side. "Hit cover, Dick!" In seconds he and Liddell were urging their steeds up the scree to the cover of the higher trees. They just made it as the posse came through the cleft below them.

Pulling in and turning his horse Liddell rubbed his bare, wiry arm as he watched. The whole of his body was lean-structured, and what was exposed was deeply weathered, so much so that the tattoos on his arms were almost obliterated. As he leant forward and peered down, two chains, each festooned with rings, dangled from his neck. Some rings held stones, or had holes where stones had been. All the rings were blackened, like the exposed areas of his flesh, weathered by the sun. Each ring, and there were many, was from a woman whom he had loved and left. So he said.

"Think they see'd us?" he asked, leaning forward under the branches and stroking the side of his mount's neck to ensure it stayed quiet.

"We'll soon know."

The lawmen passed, continuing into the distance without a glance in their direction.

"What the hell they come back for?" Clements said. The skin of his face was shiny-red and pockmarked. He had to keep out of the sun; otherwise his skin just reddened; sometimes he envied the deep tan of his comrade. "They're empty-handed, that's for sure. Ain't got Cary or the bounty."

"Maybe they didn't catch up with the stage."

"They caught up with it all right. A team of mules hauling half a ton of stage don't stand much chance against plain horsemen."

"So what happened?"

"Only one thing. They reached the stage but Cary wasn't on it."

"How come? We know the bounty booked passage clear to Junction City."

"That bounty is one smart butternut. He's made a show of leaving town by stage — and somehow switched to horses."

Liddell lit up a smoke and drew deep. He smoked so much, the fingers of his right hand would be nicotine-brown even without the sun. "What do we do now?"

"It's getting dark, so we best rest up. Then we carry on."

"Hell, this is turning into nothing but a blind chase."

"So what? There's enough at stake."

So there was. Over forty thousand dollars deposited in the Pasco Mercantile Bank, Kansas. Forty thousand of the James gang's loot, deposited under a fictitious name. Clean money, untouchable, safe. Until some little pissant of a teller embezzled fifty thousand. He hadn't cleared the place out but the company was so small his action had enforced the closure of the bank so that no depositor could withdraw. Honest and dishonest depositors alike were affected. Huh, the friggin' son-of-a-bitch wouldn't even know he'd heisted James gang money! Deposited by none other than Jesse himself.

At its height there'd been fourteen members in the joint James-Younger gang. But after the Northfield set-up there were few left who weren't on a life or six feet under. There was Jesse and Frank. And others, less than you could count on one hand, all in hiding, scattered to all points of three states.

Including the two men peering from the high trees at the Jefferson Springs posse disappear into the distance: Arch Clements and Dick Liddell.

To them and Jesse, it might not have really mattered who got their hands on Cary — the law or them. Just as long as the stolen money — or most of it — was located. But there were two flies in the can of ointment that Cary had opened. One, the boys were getting mighty low on funds. Jesse had been their funnel for money. All he'd had to do was go down to the bank in his respectable suit and withdraw whatever was wanted. There'd been ample for Jesse, Arch, Dick and the two Ford brothers who had been lying low. Now the honey-pot was gone. Secondly, they were all worried that the robbery could lead to questions being asked about the depositors. Attention might be attracted to the biggest account of all, putting Jesse, albeit with an alias, in the limelight. That kind of scrutiny he could do without.

The surviving members of the James gang were active men; they couldn't just sit around and wait for the law to take its course, so slow it might not even recover the funds. They were itchy and had to deal themselves into the play.

That way they might even take the money for themselves. Although they hadn't voiced it, that was a thought that had occurred to both of them.

8

ANOTHER early start, wash, shave, breakfast in the semi-darkness. Then Jonathan Grimm made his way to Knox Creek's one and only livery stable. The ostler was not yet about so he went through to the stalls without disturbing the man. Glad to see his master, the Andalusian emptied himself on the straw in excitement before he could get him outside. They'd been together a long time and the horse had seen him through many scrapes. Once, when he had a commission to clean up Arizona in preparation for its achieving statehood, the animal had carried him from one end of the state to the other. But they'd both been younger then.[1]

---

[1] This period of Grimm's life is recorded in 'GUNS OF THE REAPER' published by Robert Hale.

The grey was skittish as Grimm led him from the stall and outside for some air. After he'd had a little exercise running round the corral Grimm calmed him and guided him back to the centre of the stable. Facing the entrance he heaved up his saddle and gently lowered it onto the horse's back. His old joints creaked as he bent to fix the cinch.

"I knew it wouldn't be long, Jonathan," he heard a voice say. He straightened up and looked across the horse's back. At the entrance there was a man's figure silhouetted against the morning sun. The voice continued, "As soon as I saw the horse, I said to myself: there's only one man this side of the Appalachians got a bronc like that. I'd know that grey anywhere. Ain't no other like it. If ever you wanna do a deal on him . . ."

Grimm knew the voice and shape even though the features were indistinct. Lee Hammersley. "Morning, Lee. Cut the small-talk. What is it?"

The rival bounty-hunter had his arm fully extended from the shoulder aiming an ugly-looking Smith & Wesson across the back of the horse. "Just a matter of being up early and waiting," Hammersley went on.

"Spit it out," Grimm said. "You ain't making no social call. You know the two of us have nothing to do with each other in the social sphere. Whenever our trails cross, it's business. What's on your mind?"

"Horatio Cary. That's what. I been on his trail for four weeks. I finally trace the bozo and — bingo — you snap the cuffs on him."

"Luck of the draw, Lee."

"Like Sacramento?"

The Reaper shook his head. "When I picked up Duffy McCloud I didn't even know he'd escaped from you."

"Well, he had. I got him first."

"Lee, you know it's the one who takes 'em that counts." Grimm paused and shrugged. "Okay. If you can put a case that your initial capturing of him helped me by delaying him, I'm willing to discuss some arrangement on the bounty."

"No. That's chicken-feed. I want Cary."

Grimm turned more serious. "You got a gun pointing at me, Lee. You know I don't cotton to that."

"Oh, you've noticed?"

Cary, aroused by the increasingly loud interchange of words, had appeared in the hotel doorway and was observing develoments from a safe distance.

"You've never drawn on me before," Grimm went on. "You'd shoot me?"

"Not to kill, if I could help it. But you know me, Jonathan. I don't cock a hammer less'n I'm serious."

"You can't be sure of hitting me."

"No. I agree. Probably hit the horse. Your beloved Andalusian. You wouldn't like that. We wouldn't like it. But, like they say, you can't make an omelette without breaking an egg!"

Grimm was fully aware that he could take some protection from the horse.

But it was true that the notion was abhorrent to him.

"We've all got our faults, Jonathan. One of yours is you and that horse. It's your trademark, gives you away anywhere. And you'd take any crud rather than see harm come to him." Hammersley hadn't noticed that Grimm had not yet fixed the cinch. Nor did he see Grimm's hands behind the horse moving slowly inwards, to grip the extremities of the saddle. Without warning he upended the thing, flipping it towards his adversary.

Hammersley fired but his bullet sank into leather. The explosion prompted the horse to launch forward and, as the gap between them cleared, Grimm leapt at waist-level, knocking Hammersley to the ground. He gripped the pistol-wrist with his left hand just as the gun fired again. The bullet disappeared into the roof as Grimm crashed his right fist against the man's jaw. Despite his age, the Reaper still had a helluva punch and for a few seconds Hammersley didn't know what time of year it was. When he came to, Grimm was standing with his own gun levelled.

There was indecision in Hammersley's eyes. Should he try something or not?

"Don't think I wouldn't do it, pal," the Reaper said, shaking his gun menacingly. "Knowing you could shoot me has lowered my inhibitions. Now get up and haul ass to the law office."

"What you gonna cite against me? These local hicks ain't gonna be concerned with a conflict of interest between you and me!"

"You must have come into town later than me so that it was too dark for you to read the notice."

"What notice, you son-of-a-bitch?"

"There's a strict bye-law here about firing weapons within town limits!"

The object of their common interest, the timid Mr Cary, had left the confines of the hotel porch and now hesitantly followed them at some distance down the street.

"If it ain't me," Hammersley said as they heavy-footed in their riding-boots along the boardwalk, "it'll be somebody else who'll stop you getting Cary to Kansas,"

"Open season, is it?"

"You'd be surprised how many bodies have got an interest in the man. For a start, the law from Jefferson Springs is after him. A whole posse of 'em. You can't take them on."

Grimm ignored his words and knocked on the law office door.

Five minutes later, he and Cary were heading back to the hotel. The sheriff had been somewhat digruntled at being woken early by gunfire, and, taking the word of Cary as a witness, had locked up Hammersley for the rest of the day for breaking the town ordinance on use of guns.

"Why didn't you run?" Grimm asked. "You had the chance."

"Because I'm aware that you're far more experienced at chasing and catching than I am at running."

"And why did you back me with the sheriff? When Hammersley started quibbling it was your being a witness that helped put the critter in the slammer and out of my hair for a spell."

"From what I gleaned from the conversation between the two of you, I'd rather take my chances with you than him. At the moment it has to be one or the other. I figured better the devil I know, than the devil I don't."

Grimm pondered on the words as they stepped onto the boardwalk. "You said — at the moment?"

"Oh, I'm going to make a dash for it, Mr Grimm. There is no option. But I am conservative by profession. I shall only leave your company when an opportunity arises in which I judge the odds are greatly in my favour."

Grimm smiled. "That's honest at least."

Just before they reached the hotel Grimm noticed a stage loading up at the end of town. He paused on the boardwalk and thought about the equine incompetence of his prisoner.

"You get on upstairs," he said to Cary when they were inside the small foyer of the hotel, "and finish getting ready to leave." Cary did as he was bid while Grimm himself lit up his pipe and waited in the foyer. Wreathed in smoke and occasionally glancing up and down the street, he looked like some sagebrush philosopher reflecting on the dawning of a new day. Actually he was waiting for the last of the rubbernecking busybodies, attracted by the ruckus, to disappear. When there was no-one left on the street he moved briskly down the thoroughfare to the stage. It was a roughly-hewn box shape with its door at the rear.

"Where you headed?" he asked the driver, who was adjusting the harnesses.

"Brownsburg."

Grimm closed his eyes while he sorted out the geography in his mind. "North-east, ain't it?"

"Was last time we went, pardner."

The compass-bearing was not the best — but good enough. "When you leaving?"

"Soon as we can shove off. We're late already."

"You got two seats?"

"Sure. But I ain't waiting."

"That's okay by me. I want to leave town as soon as possible without being seen." Grimm had been thinking aloud and immediately realized he shouldn't have added the last bit.

The driver looked apprehensive. "Without being seen? You ain't got the law after you, have you? I don't want no trouble, mister."

Grimm shook his head and forced a chuckle. "Don't worry, pal. I ain't broke no laws."

9

UNLIKE the previous conveyance they had used out of Jefferson Springs this one was specifically designed for the transport of toilers and moilers. The door was at the rear with an aisle running the length of the vehicle with benches on either side. The interior was rough wood with no padding and there was straw on the floor. Two farmers were in deep discussion over the problems of making a living on hard-scrabble plots while three cowhands played cards across the aisle. Jonathan Grimm sat with closed eyes, his head against the rest, trying to ignore them all.

His mind moved from one thing to another. The journey for example. It sure-fire was not as the crow flies. Plotting it on the map, he mused, would show it to have more the contours of a hog's leg. Nevertheless, we are moving slowly but inexorably in the right direction. He thought of his prisoner. Well-mannered, intelligent, quiet. Not like the usual rabble he brought in for his money. He thought of the Andalusian and how he'd made sure the ostler knew how he felt about the horse before leaving it at the livery. He didn't like to leave him but it was for the best.

Then his thoughts turned to Hammersley. Would the bummaroo take up the chase again and try another snatch? Probably. He seemed quite incensed about that Sacramento business. But at least, Grimm had a twenty four hour start on him. The bozo was more of a nuisance than a threat — like summer flies round a horse's ass.

"I ain't going back until I got Cary." Sheriff Banner was running his finger along the grain of the bar top. He and his posse were taking a rest and refreshment in a saloon after trailing their quarry to Knox Creek.

"There's a limit to how much effort you put into chasing a bozo like this," one of them said. "He's only thieved a few dollars from old man Eaton. Hell, Sam, you know old Josey's not a poor man — he's a lawyer! Makes more in a week than you and me in a season."

"That ain't the point," Banner snapped.

"Anyways, sheriff, now Cary's out of the county you've done your duty by informing other law authorities about what he's done and where he's headed."

"It's the principle," Banner snorted. "No pen-pusher and two-bit bounty-hunter are gonna run rings round me."

"Principle, my ass," another grunted. "Since when have you had principles? Don't think nobody knows about the extras you get."

"Dunno what you're rattling about," Banner said.

"It's the election, ain't it?" the strong-minded one continued. "You gotta whitewash yourself, ain't yuh? After you fouled up with the town council over your cousin Biff."

"Shaddap!" the sheriff said, slamming back his drink.

"And you're trying to do it at our expense. We all got jobs to go to. We ain't paid lawmen like you. And we don't get kickbacks."

"You wanna go," the sheriff said, pouring himself another shot, "you go. Anytime, kiddo."

There was a lull until another said more calmly, "You gotta face it, boss, you're now beyond your area of jurisdiction anyhows."

The sheriff straightened up. "Once we get our paws on Cary no county lawman is gonna interfere with us taking him into custody and hauling him back to the Springs. We got the one chance. The stage that bounty's took is only a short-haul local job and takes a long, rambling route. We can easy head it off and be waiting for it when it rolls into Brownsburg."

"They might have jumped again, boss. Anywhere between here and Brownsburg."

Banner stood up, looked at the door through which he was now going to stride, and screwed his army cap firmly on his head. "I don't think he's had time to make the arrangements. Those that's still with me, let's move. Let's nail the bastard."

"You like pigs, mister?"

Jonathan Grimm shrugged. "Ain't given it much thought."

The coach had been following a corkscrew route, stopping at varied spreads and there had been much coming and going of passengers. Grimm had noted several things about the present questioner since he had boarded half an hour previously and taken a seat opposite. His slight frame was no more than five foot and sheathed in a one-piece overall indicating he was some kind of land-worker. He had slit, sunken eyes and the little hair he had around the circumference of his bald head was long and matted. An extended, wispy moustache decorated his mouth. But most of all there was the smell.

"Yeah, but I asked if you like pigs," the man repeated.

Pigs! That explained what was hitting his nostrils.

"Must admit," Grimm added, "ain't had much experience with the critters." He chuckled. "Leastways, not the animal kind. Human pigs, yeah." He lit up his pipe in an attempt to counteract the odour.

The man shook his head. "Never understood why folk use the noble hog in that way. You know, to say bad things about folks, they compare 'em to pigs."

Grimm didn't push the conversation.

"Josh Hendersen," the little man persisted and stuck out a dry but soiled hand. It was caked with something

Grimm didn't like to consider. So he just touched his hat. "Howdy."

"In time I'm gonna have the biggest hog-spread this side of Brownsburg," the man went on.

Grimm looked across at Cary. There was a grin on the pen-pusher's face which said 'It's your conversation feller, not mine'.

From that point on the bounty-hunter closed his eyes while, unperturbed by lack of audience, the man called Hendersen rambled on about his hogs, his smallholding, his plans. Matters were made worse by his local drawl that made it difficult for anyone who didn't live within a ten mile radius of the locality to understand the finer points of his droning monologue.

"Anyways, some bastard's been rustling 'em. That's why I'm going to Brownsburg. Report it to the marshal."

Grimm wondered how the hell you could get away with rustling hogs and, as a diversion, mused on the practicalities. All that grunting would surely cause attention? And how do you get a herd of hogs moving? On his understanding they weren't the fastest of God's critters. But he voiced none of these questions. In fact he found the man's drone quite soporific and conducive to dozing.

So much so, they were approaching the outskirts of Brownsburg before he knew it.

Then the coach was creaking to a standstill and the driver pulling on the brake. Steam rose from the mules and their harnesses jingled as they stamped the ground as though in disbelief that they had finally stopped. First out was the hog man, hotfooting it to the marshal's office to register his complaint about the great pig-heist. Then, one by one the other workmen-passengers emerged until at last Cary stepped down with Grimm behind him.

Before the surprised bounty-hunter could resist there was a gun-barrel hard against his stomach and men were behind him pulling his guns from their holsters.

"Welcome to Brownsburg," Banner said, his own guns, like those of the rest of his posse, levelled at Grimm and his charge. Satisfaction shone from the lawman's Messianic features. "I figured you'd be riding in on this crate. Jeez, what a smell." He hefted his gun to draw more attention to the weapon. "As long as you don't make no trouble, this is gonna be quick and painless. Irrespective of why you are holding Cary, we are relieving you of the responsibility. We're taking him because we give higher priority to getting him back to Jefferson Springs to face a charge of theft there, than whatever he's wanted for in Kansas." He motioned down the street. "Our horses are yonder. Bounty, you stay with us a piece so we can keep our eyes on you. Now, both of you, move."

Slowly the group moved down the street. It had been a busy thoroughfare until the guns had come out. Wagons and buggies were parked here and there outside of stores but passers-by were now standing transfixed, taking in the drama. The group were just approaching their horses at a hitch-rail when a harsh voice rang out. "Drop your guns, sheriff! This is the marshal of Brownsburg."

Chins dropping in surprise they all stopped and looked across the street. On the boardwalk was a man with a badge pinned to his chest and a long-barrelled repeater aimed their way. "This is my bailiwick, Banner. You ain't got no jurisdiction here and you ain't taking nobody no place until we got this matter sorted out."

"He's right, boss," Banner's sidekick muttered. "I told you we ain't got no jurisdiction."

"Shut your face," Banner hissed.

"And before you get any funny ideas," the first speaker continued, "that's my dep behind you."

Banner turned and faced another gun

barrel with another man and badge behind it.

"Now drop your weapons like I said," the first man went on. "Then hand over Cary and everything will be honky-dory."

It intrigued Grimm that the lawman should know Cary by name but at the moment he was passive in the proceedings.

"Okay," Banner said to his men. "He's got the drop on us anyways."

They were just about to comply when there was a shout from further down the street. "That ain't the marshal!"

Everyone turned to see a little man in dirty overalls running along the boardwalk. It was the hog man who'd come to town to report his stolen pigs. "I've just looked through the law office window!" he shouted, coming to a standstill at a safe distance. "The marshal and his deputy are out cold and trussed up like turkey-cocks!"

The men in the centre of the street dived to the ground or for the cover of parked vehicles as gunfire erupted. Chunks splintered from woodwork on all sides as shots were exchanged. Suddenly the Banner man who had been holding the bounty-hunter's guns fell backwards moaning. Grimm leapt across and retrieved his fallen weapons.

"Come on," he shouted at Cary. "Keep low and follow me." They loped down the boardwalk and into an alley. Grimm proned himself against the wall and cautiously peered back round the corner. The two riflemen were pinning Banner's men down. It seemed incredible that only two men could neutralize a posse of lawmen. But, apart from Banner, the posse was made up of part-time amateurs and the two men on the prod had repeaters and knew how to use them.

They were professional gunmen all right but who the hell were they? He had no idea, but that wasn't important now. "Come on," he ordered Cary again and loped down the alley. There was a buckboard standing at the rear of a hardware store. It had been in the process of being loaded when the ruckus had started but now stood unattended as the workmen had gone back through the store, attracted by the noise. Grimm pulled Cary up with him onto the seat, kicked off the brake and urged forward the two-horse team. Unseen, they sped along the backway, then out of town, sacks of animal feed bouncing about on the back.

Gradually the crackle of gunfire faded to their rear but the Reaper didn't let up until Brownsburg was miles behind and out of sight. "Any idea who those bush-whackers were?" he said as his breath returned. "They sure-fire weren't law."

"No, sir. Never seen them before."

"There's somebody else after you. Hammersley said something about that. You know of anybody else? Or any reason why they should have an interest in you?"

Cary was still gripping the bouncing vehicle. "No, sir."

Despite the trouble the little fellow was causing him, Grimm had developed some liking for him. And believed him when he said he didn't know what the ruckus was all about. For someone who had heisted over fifty thousand dollars he sure was an innocent.

There are more things in heaven and earth, Horatio, than are dreamt of in your philosophy," Grimm grunted, flicking the ribbons for a little more speed.

"What was that, sir?"

"Shakespeare."

"Come again, sir?"

"Never mind."

10

AWAY from established trail, they crossed a stretch of prairie, the smell of the land rising from the crushed soil under the horses' hooves. Way back, Grimm had dropped the sacks of feed off the back to lighten the load. Eventually, at the top of a grade, he halted the wagon in the lee of a boulder. He didn't want to hinder their progress but there were the horses to think of.

"You got no idea who pulled that stunt back there?" he asked. "Those bozos masquerading as the law?"

"No, sir. Never seen them before."

"Well, they knew you all right. Called you by name. You upset anybody?"

"No, sir."

Grimm lit his pipe while he pondered on the matter. That was a stupid thing for him to have asked. You don't steal fifty thousand dollars without upsetting somebody! "They wouldn't be Pinkertons," he mused. "Pinks wouldn't make a play like that."

It had to remain a puzzle and shortly they were rolling again. Grimm was deliberately keeping off the trail, maintaining an easterly bearing. He didn't like doing it in a wagon not built for rough terrain but there was nothing for it. The going was bad. It had been getting worse from where they had stopped and it got increasingly uneven. Suddenly there was a crunch and the wagon dipped, slewing to a halt. Grimm dropped down and checked. The front wheel had hit a rock and a handful of spokes were shattered.

"Judas Priest," he muttered. Exasperated and indecisive, he considered the terrain ahead. Nothing but a lot more of the same. For a moment he thought of riding the horses, but they were all lathered up now and Cary wouldn't stay long on a bare back. Would probably complain about walking, too, but he didn't ask him. He unharnessed the animals and scatted them with his hat. "They can find their own way home." Then he began to walk east. "Come on, Horatio. Let's wear out some shoe-leather."

Grimm stood on the riverbank studying the breadth of water flowing before him, blocking their passage east. "Figure it's a tributary of the Kansas River," he said, more to himself than to Cary who had just trudged up and joined him. Nearer its source than the mighty river that it eventually fed into, it did not display a full force. However, it was formidable enough: there must have been rain in the north as it was running high. Nevertheless, had he been alone, Grimm would have still considered swimming it. "I suppose you're gonna tell me you can't swim either," he continued.

"That's right, sir. Water terrifies me."

"How did I guess?" The bounty-hunter breathed dismissively. He looked up and down the river. To the south in the distance, there appeared to be a building by the riverside. "Could be a crossing-point," he guessed. "Come on, pal, let's head downstream."

They progressed along the riverbank and, as they neared, they could see he had been right in his conjecture. There was a shack on either side and they had been built where cottonwoods were on adjacent banks, so the giant trees could be used to fix the ferry's lines. On their approach they were greeted by the ferryman, young and eager to please. The ferry was moored on the nearside and the boatman was carrying sapling-trunks from it, stacking them near the building. Grimm nodded in acceptance when the man told him the toll and he stepped onto the wooden boards with Cary. The ferry-man had been fetching the timber from the other side of the river, because there was an axe and a few trunks still on the boat.

The man unhooked the couplings, jumped onto the raft and pulled up the board. He started cranking a handle so that the cable, which stretched across the water, whipped tight and the flat-bottomed craft began to move. He was an expert at working his equipment and minutes later they had nearly completed the full span. "Looks like I got some customers for the return trip," he said cheerfully as they neared the landing-stage. Two men had appeared from behind the far shack. They were standing awkwardly, each with a hand behind his back.

"Yeah," the barquero continued, "I recognize 'em. I took 'em across earlier in the day."

Grimm didn't like their cut. Then he knew why. They were the two who had posed as lawmen at Brownsburg and had started shooting up the place! His taking a detour from the main trail and the accident forcing him to walk made it no puzzle how they'd got ahead. And he was even more interested in their identity now they had the drop on him with those damned long-arms they suddenly pulled from behind their backs and levelled.

"Reverse," he grunted to the ferryman as soon as he saw the guns. "Pronto. No questions." The ferryman did as he was bid but was halted by a slug splintering the wheel-mounting.

"No you don't!" one of the men barked. "Keep it coming, ferryman, if you want to keep that head on your shoulders. You, bounty, drop your gunbelt. Then grab for sky."

Between Grimm and the gunnies there was a chest-high board that could be hinged down for the passage of wagons and horses; but from this distance the hardcases' slugs would rip straight through the wood like cardboard. Judas Priest, he never liked being stripped of his weapons but at the moment he had no option. If the gunnies started shooting at least one of the men on the raft would catch some lead. He paused but was prompted by another slug pinging off a metal joint.

"Okay," he said. "No need to waste

your ammo." Being denuded of his hardware was sure becoming a habit. He untied the holster-strings around his legs, unclipped the buckle of his gunbelt and lowered his gun-rig to the wooden boards as the raft creaked towards the desperadoes.

"Hold it, ferryman!" a voice suddenly said from behind, the words bouncing across the water. "And start turning back." What the hell . . . ? Grimm looked over his shoulder and saw the black-clad Lee Hammersley on the bank behind him with his Winchester up to his eye!

"Dive for cover!" Grimm shouted and hit the planking. The other two aboard the craft followed suit as an exchange of gunfire erupted between Hammersley, now behind one of the mooring cottonwoods, and the two gunnies.

Grimm picked up the ferryman's axe from the timber pile. Keeping knees bent to give himself some protection, he began swinging at the ropes. Splinters flew from the wooden board as one of the gunnies turned his attention back to the ferryboat.

One, two chops, and the main cable was severed. He scuttled across and began hacking at the second. Freed from one rope, the ferryboat began to swing a little downstream, revealing one of the unprotected sides to the gunnies. Grimm had just managed to weaken the rope with one slice before the gunnies could take advantage of it when a bullet spanged off the blade, juddering it out of his hands and sending him to the floor. He tried to rise but the boat had swung right round so they were now in full view of the attackers and another bullet scored his arm. At that time the little pen-pusher came to life, jumping up and scampering across the boards. He picked up the axe and started to work, albeit clumsily, with bullets whistling round him.

"Well I'll be . . . ," Grimm exclaimed, gripping his arm and watching the man struggling with the axe. It was probably the heaviest thing he'd ever picked up in his life.

Finally the connection was sliced and Cary dropped down.

"You okay, Mr Grimm?" he said, crawling across the boards and looking at the rent in the bounty-hunter's sleeve.

Grimm touched it and saw a smear of blood on his fingers. "Yeah. It ain't done no damage. You okay?"

"Yes, sir. But damn scared!"

The second severed cable had whipped back — but the loose end had snagged in the corner of the woodwork and the ferry began to curve round in an arc, back towards the starting side.

Keeping under cover of trees and firing spasmodically, Hammersley was moving along the riverbank keeping level with the free-wheeling craft. He saw the ferry crunch against the side.

"Come on out of there, Jonathan!" he barked, with the ferry now transfixed against the bank by the current and trapped rope. "Quick. And bring Cary."

Grimm ignored the bounty-hunter's order and picked up one of his guns. "Cut that fixing," he said to Cary as he turned his back on Hammersley and took a couple of shots himself at the two riflemen. The little man started chopping at the snagged cable but just as he cut it, Hammersley slithered down the bank and dropped heavy-footed onto the boards. "You ain't losing me that fast, Jonathan," he grunted up close, ramming his Winchester hard into Grimm's back. "Not now I've saved your hide. Now put down your iron."

Grimm complied. "They wouldn't have killed me," he added, in an attempt to escape the debt. "It's Cary they're after."

"Anyways, who are they?"

"Beats me. Cary says he doesn't know."

"Makes no never mind. Cary's mine now." Hammersley kept his Winchester pointing at Grimm's belly. "Drop that axe, Cary. And you, Jonathan, back off, away from your guns." He snatched a glance back upstream. The two gunslingers had mounted up and were hell-batting along the bank, reducing the distance between them. Once more bullets began cutting wood and pinging off metal.

"Like hell they won't kill you," Hammersley grinned, letting off a shot over the board.

"Let me have my guns, Lee," Grimm said. "We can handle 'em together."

"No. Jus' keep low and you'll be safe." Then he laughed. "See!" The riders had suddenly hit another tributary blocking their path, flowing heavy, providing no chance of passage. He watched them sitting astride their broncs in frustration at the water's edge, getting smaller as the loose ferry whirled along in the current. Then he pulled himself up and sat on a corner-top, wedging his boots against the boards so he had vantage of the river while keeping the three men aboard at gunpoint. "Now those two bozos are out of our hair," he said, "all we gotta do is wait until we fetch up against a side and we can pull in."

The river flow was even stronger now that it had been joined by another tributary, but it was fairly even so, although the raft yawed and rolled slightly, it was without danger. As Hammersley said, at the moment there was little they could do but wait until they neared a bank or made shallow water.

"You know, I'm beginning to enjoy this caper, Jonathan," Hammersley said. "There's not only money at the end of the day but there's been fun along the way." He got no further; his delight was short-lived. The raft juddered as it hit an underwater obstacle. While the three standing men were hurled to the floor under the impetus, Hammersley was pitched into the water as the boat stopped unexpectedly. His arms flailed as he tried to fight the current. Meanwhile the raft snagged for a moment, spun round and fetched up in the shallows near a bank. Grimm picked up his guns and watched his rival bounty-hunter disappearing fast into the distance.

"So long, Lee."

Cary ran to the side of the boat, concern in his eyes.

"Don't worry, Horatio, he can swim," the Reaper chuckled. "I hope."

He looked over the side and could see the bottom under a foot of water. He climbed over the rail and jumped in. The other two followed him in, wading to the side. On dry land, Cary helped Grimm ease off his jacket.

"Just as I thought," the bounty-hunter said after a brief inspection of the wound. "Just a graze. But damned sore."

"No need for that," he added when he saw the large handkerchief Cary had pulled out of his pocket.

"I insist. It's for the best."

After Cary had fixed the makeshift bandage and helped him to don his jacket again Grimm looked about him as he swung his belt around his hips and fastened the buckle. Nearby there was a cottonwood stump that looked like it had been struck by lightning. "I'll help you tie up to that bole," he said to the ferryman. "That way you save your ferry."

As the man returned to his craft for a coil of rope, Grimm looked up and down the river. For the time being they were safe both from the gunslingers and Hammersley. But both were still unknown quantities and he knew in time they were likely to turn up anywhere. So he added, "Then we gotta git."

The ferryman tied the rope to a stanchion on the boat and threw the end to Grimm who took it to the tree-stump. "How does one get east from here?" he asked after he'd knotted the rope.

"Well, the railroad's making headway

into the state. Hear tell it's got as far as Angel Bluff."

"And how does one get to Angel Bluff?"

"Well, downstream a piece there's a bridge. If it's still standing! Then maybe it's ten or fifteen miles east of the crossing."

Grimm shrugged. "I'm beholden to yuh." He flipped a couple of double eagles to the young man. Sorry about the trouble we caused you and your boat. And I'd be obliged if you didn't tell anybody about where we're heading." He grinned as he nodded his head for Cary to start walking. "Not that my asking folks to keep quiet seems to be making much difference!"

11

THEY trudged over meadows having followed the river to the bridge and crossed to the east. Then, pastureland and fields of fresh, red soil. Grass gave way to scrub, scrub to bracken. Then grass again. They passed a small group of Indians. Kansa Indians, the 'people of the south wind', after whom the state was named. Grimm waved but made no contact. They were a sorry-looking sight, homeless, doomed, their ancestral lands diminishing with Kansas being put to cattle and the plough.

The two men plodded on, sagebrush and sunflowers underfoot. They made their way through fields of corn, from time to time sighting men and women harvesting in the distance. The heads of the corn were hanging, showing the berries were heavy, making for good quality wheat. That was Kansas's future, a future in which there was little role for Indians. Or bounty-hunters.

For a long time they didn't see another human being until they spied a tinker with an old nag pulling a red wagon clanking with pots and pans, crossing their path ahead of them. He pulled in and waited till they caught up, watching them with piercing eyes under unbroken, bushy eyebrows that crossed his forehead in a single span.

Relishing the chance of some contact, he checked that they were thirsty and amenable to some frontier conviviality over coffee.

"Sure could use some of that," Grimm said, taking off his hat and wiping the wind-blown chaff from his neck. The tinker scuttled round the back of his vehicle to extract a little stove and in a short time he'd got coffee bubbling. The foot-sloggers appreciated the break in their trek and the three sat in the shade of the wagon with their drinks.

"Yes, sirree," the old man said in answer to a question by the bounty-hunter. "Railroad should be over that way a-piece." He waved his arm vaguely and chuckled a toothless cackle. "But don't pay too much mind to old Matthew. I've lost my own trail."

Grimm groaned inwardly. The old guy had lost a few marbles along the way, too. "What trail's that, pardner?" he said.

"The northern trail." The tinker's crag-face, with features sculpted in walnut by years of headwinds, cracked apart and he cackled again. "Huh, don't even know what state I'm in!"

"Figure you're in Kansas," Grimm said, throwing away most of his vile-tasting coffee.

The tinker touched his nose as though imparting a secret and winked. But there was a touch of madness in the eyes. "Hear tell a body can make a fortune with cooking-utensils and the like up in the goldfields. Can sell 'em for top dollar. That's what

I'm gonna do. None of that panning for old Matthew."

Grimm thanked him — at least the few sips had slaked his thirst — and the two could hear his mad cackle for a long time behind them as they resumed their journey.

It was much later that they saw what seemed to be a building in the distance. Plodding along, heads down with tiredness, seeing little but dirt passing beneath their feet, it was a wonder they saw it from so far away. When they got close they could see it was not a building but an old wheel-less passenger car. But closer still, it transpired to be a welcome marker, with ANGEL BLUFF painted in crude lettering on its side, standing close to the railroad. A rabbit was going about his business in the open and looked in surprise at the approaching intruders, then made for sanctuary between the wheel-springs in the undergrowth that had developed under the car. So much for the station. At least it would provide shade and if there was a rabbit there wouldn't be any snakes. Miraculously there were a few panes of glass, opaque with dirt, in the windows.

Brackish water lay at the bottom of a rusting tank and Grimm stopped the thirsty Cary from sampling it. "All right for hosses," he said. "See if you can pull any water from that thing," he suggested, indicating an ancient pump. While Cary cranked away behind him he looked inside the car. Wooden veneer had long lost its shine and discoloured brass fittings hung broken. "An agreeable hostelry", he said to himself as he stepped in and inspected more closely. Seats were worn and ripped, horse-hair stuffing ballooning out. But a few were serviceable. What upholstery there was was dusty; and dirt crunched underfoot as he walked down the aisle. It was undisturbed and that was good. Any snakes in residence would have left coiling-marks. Ever since the little escapade approaching Jefferson Springs he'd been getting a thing about the scaly critters.

He went outside as Cary managed to get some water flowing. Grimm cupped a hand under the stream and sniffed at it. Seemed okay. Better than old Matthew's coffee. They took it in turns to pull some for each other. Then the bounty-hunter scouted around. There was a pair of rusting wheels connected by an axle. "Help me roll these onto the track," he said. "There's no signal but this'll stop any through trains."

They heaved the things into place and returned to the passenger car.

"Give me your boots," Grimm said. "Just a precaution," he explained as he took them from the bankteller and selected a seat which was still relatively intact. An old, leather luggage-case lay, open, dusty and cobwebby, once the holder of someone's dreams. He pushed it aside, sat down and pulled off his own boots, groaning in appreciation.

He stacked the two pairs at the end of a seat and lay down with his head on the footwear, shifting his body to make himself comfortable. He read the small enamel sign directly opposite him requesting PLEASE DO NOT SPIT, and closed his eyes. "That was a brave thing you did back there on the ferry," he said after a while. "Cutting the cable in full view of those big galoots with the pea-shooters."

Cary took the compliment without comment.

"You're full of surprises," Grimm went on, tiredness reflecting in his lazy drone.

Cary settled on another seat. "I surprised myself when I took that money from the Pasco bank in the first place. Ain't done nothing like that in my whole life. My folks were Methodists and that's the way I've always tried to be. My old man would turn over in his grave if he knew what I been and done."

"Then why did you steal it?"

"The owner of the bank was planning to set his son on. It was only

126

a small operation and there wasn't enough business for two tellers. Then I overheard him talking to one of his business cronies from town about giving me the can. Me! I'd worked for the bastard — excuse me for fifteen years." He chuckled. "I kinda acted before he did."

A jay landed on a window-frame, saw the place was occupied and flew away with a chirrup.

"That woman back there," Grimm said. "What was her name? Mrs van Damm, that was it. She your accomplice?"

"Accomplice? What do you mean?"

"You and she seemed pretty close. Was she holing you up until the heat was off?"

Cary chuckled. "No. She didn't know anything about the bank business until you showed up."

"You got something going with her?"

"What does that mean?"

"We're talking turkey for Christ's sake. She your woman?"

Cary chuckled again without humour. "Seemed she got plans for the two of us if that's what you mean. But she didn't tell me about them until you put those irons on me. Then it was kinda too late."

Jonathan Grimm sighed like he was in an impasse. "Look, in my sphere of operation you don't say sorry. It's an attitude that comes with the territory. But, if you did, I'd say it now."

There was silence for a spell. "Back to your exploits with the axe," the bounty-hunter went on. "Why'd you do it? There was no need for you to risk anything. You're piggy-in-the-middle in this game."

I don't know. Impulse, I suppose."

"Well, thanks. You feel like being impulsive in the future you go ahead."

"My next impulse might be to scoot."

It was Grimm's turn to leave a comment hanging in mid-air and he pulled his stetson over his eyes. "Let me know when a train arrives."

12

IT was the long whistle that woke him. He looked out of one of the windows. Good. The train was going in the right direction. They pulled on their boots and by the time the locomotive rolled in they had pulled the wheels off the tracks.

The black grimness of the machine was alien in the clean, green faraway place yet its oily, steaming presence gave meaning to the desolate railroad halt. They strode past the snorting locomotive, its firebox soul glowing, and stepped up into a carriage. The conductor was already waiting for them at the end of the aisle, puffing his cheeks and agitatedly moving his head. "We're behind time. We shouldn't really be stopping here."

Grimm felt like saying "What the hell are trains for?" but paid the fares without comment and soon they were moving. The main traffic for the line was incoming settlers so the train now journeying east had few passengers and the two men had an end section of a car to themselves.

"I suppose you see your job as doing good," Cary said after a while, gazing at the prairie flashing by. After their sleep at the halt they were both wide-awake.

"Nope. Do it for the money. Pure and simple."

"So you have no principles."

"I didn't say that."

"No, but that's what you mean. What principles can a man have, who lives by the gun and outside the law?"

"Just 'cause I don't carry a badge, don't mean I'm outside the law. Anyway, I got a few principles."

"Name one."

This conversation wasn't Grimm's style but he felt he had to humour the man. "Okay. I'd never shoot a man in the back. Least, not an intentional killing shot. Don't seem a proper way of conducting your business. Some bounties would, but I wouldn't. I could have done many a time. In a face-up, some men just up and run. If they do that I'll give 'em a warning shot. If they carry on I might chase 'em or wing 'em. Depends on the circumstances. But I'd never kill, not in the back. Not that they don't deserve it. Many of the men I take in are no-good killers."

"Have you never killed?"

"Mr Cary, I have a rep for taking in dead men. Ain't got no qualms about putting a bullet through a black heart in a face-on draw. And I ain't been beat yet. Of course, there is some day lying ahead when I'm gonna meet my match. I'm realist enough to know that. Just hope I've got the sense and the money to have retired before that day comes. Even so, I ain't shot nobody in the back. No, sir. Call it part of my code if you like." He tamped the tobacco in his pipe, lit it and puffed. "Why all the questions about me, anyways?"

"I'd just like to know something about the man who aims to take me in."

"Listen, I *am* taking you in, no 'aiming' about it." Then there was silence between them as both watched the changing colours of the prairie. Grimm was satisfied with their progress. They were over half-way in their journey and this locomotive would pull them straight into Kansas City itself and it was moving fast.

"Anyway, talking of principles," Grimm said after a spell, "you're the villain out of the two of us. Not me. Remember that."

"Villain, Mr Grimm? All I did was take some money from a bank. A bank isn't people. Is that so bad?"

"You know, I hear that a lot in my occupation. Villains excusing their stealing from banks and railroads by saying it don't hurt nobody because they're heisting from companies — and companies ain't people. That's a loada

132

crud. All money belongs to someone. Companies are people. Investors, big and small. Besides, there are after-effects, like knocking over dominoes. One thing leads to another."

"So? I hurt a few rich people! Huh, tough!"

"A few rich people? What about all the small farmers whose life savings were in the Pasco bank? The meagre funds of little old ladies?"

"No, no, you got it wrong, Mr Grimm. There were a few small accounts, yes. I grant that. But I stole fifty thousand dollars, and forty thousand of that was one account!"

What for Grimm had been small-talk suddenly took on a new significance. There was something here that could repay being thought through. If only one person had been hurt in a big way by Horatio Cary's embezzling, that meant there was one person with one helluva grievance against the little pen-pusher. One person with enough reason to pay someone to locate Cary, to find out where he'd stashed it. Not one reason, forty thousand reasons!

That could explain those two bad-asses who were after their blood.

"You remember the name on that account?"

"Of course I do."

"What was the name, just for the record?"

Cary chuckled. "You don't get me like that. I've told you before, Mr Grimm. As long as I tell you nothing, I'm no asset to you."

Grimm shrugged and concentrated on cleaning out his pipe. Cary watched him fiddling with a little knife. First he scraped around the bowl and knocked out black debris against his heel. Then he separated the stem and started blowing down it. But there was some kind of blockage and the bounty-hunter — gaunt, serious, dedicated — suddenly took on a brief comical aspect with his cheeks ballooning and frustration in his eyes.

How could you start liking someone

whose main aim was to cold-heartedly deprive you of your liberty for financial gain? Cary couldn't answer the question but he knew for sure he had developed some liking for the man sitting opposite him, despite of everything.

Suddenly a gobbet of something execrable shot out of the end of the tube. The resulting look of unashamed relief on the bounty-hunter's face was so blatant, Cary almost burst out laughing. He contained himself while he continued to watch the man take out his pouch and meticulously fill the pipe. Then he said, "Listen, Mr Grimm. This escapade is developing a high degree of risk. There are a lot of bullets flying around."

"So?" Grimm said, striking a match.

"A veritable unhealthy element has entered the proceedings. If anything should happen to me I want you to remember something."

"Yeah?"

Cary paused before he said, "Xanadu, Falls City."

"What's that? Your home town?"

Cary didn't explain.

"You got folks there you want me to tell?" Grimm pressed.

"Just say it, so you remember it."

Grimm pensively puffed out some smoke. "Xanadu, Falls City," he said slowly.

"Okay."

The bounty-hunter looked mystified for a moment, then, realizing there was to be no explanation, tried to look disinterested by casually gazing out of the window.

They were silent again for a long time, both looking out of the window but oblivious to the passing vista, each once more occupied by his own thoughts. Then Grimm suddenly noticed something. Judas Priest! Telegraph wires. All along the side of the track, moving up and down against the window in between posts. They'd begun some distance away from Angel Bluff but they'd been there a long time now. He'd seen them but not paid them much mind. Of course, if the railroad had got this far west now, so could the telegraph. Almost mesmerized he stared at the undulating line. Up and down in waves between the posts. Would it have buzzed a message about his progress? About his location, about his being on this very train? There were so many fingers in this pie: Sheriff Banner, the two mysterious gunslingers, Hammersley, and the Pinkertons would be on the lookout. Could he assume the message had not been sent ahead? Could he complacently assume there would be no-one waiting at the next station, or the next, or the next . . . ? Dare he chance it, this close to his goal? Could he hell!

Lee Hammersley had been in the canoe for the greater part of a day and had become quite proficient. When he had stolen it from its moorings at a landing-stage it was the first time in his life he'd paddled such a craft. But he had found that, going with the current, all he had to do was guide the thing from time to time and make sure he avoided the occasional rock. He'd decided to continue downstream as opposed to walking back to the ferry-station as the flow was heading, despite its twists and turns, in an easterly direction. He knew Grimm was aiming for Kansas City and that was east. Although he was happy with his progress he knew eventually he must align himself with a more conventional route, for such would Grimm be taking, if he wanted to retain a slim chance of meeting up with him again.

It was in that regard that he was becoming increasingly concerned. The banks of the river had been rising for some time and now he was slicing the water between precipitous cliffs.

Ahead he suddenly could see something spanning the gorge, way above the water. Wooden trellis-work. A railroad bridge! He worked his way across the river and guided the canoe into a rocky inlet. Leaping out he hauled the craft clear of the eddying water and stretched his limbs, grateful to be able to stand. He looked up and assessed the climb, noting clefts in the rocky edifice. It would present no major problem in its ascent.

At the top he took in the terrain as he paused for breath. No signs of habitation, just track in both directions.

"When's the next stop?" Grimm asked the pot-bellied conductor as he moved down the aisle past the bounty-hunter's seat. The train was swaying as it lurched and creaked over a bridge. The uniformed man looked out of the window at the gorge and river below, then at his watch. "Just coming up, sir. Fifteen minutes. We can't keep this speed though; there's a grade coming up. She'll have to slow down."

"Thanks." Grimm waited until the man had passed through to the next car forward. "Come on," he said to Cary. "Let's take a walk."

"What's on your mind?"

"We need some fresh air," Grimm responded, rising and taking the shorter man's arm. "Come on."

Steadying themselves by holding rails and seats they moved back to the observation platform of the last car. There was an old lady sitting in a seat stroking a small dog on her lap.

"Ma'am," Grimm said, touching his hat. She hadn't liked this man since he'd boarded the train. Unshaven, dirty. The palest and unhealthiest face she'd ever seen. And the way he ordered the poor little man around was uncivilized. She didn't reply but left her side of the conversation to the dog, who echoed her sentiments by snapping at the bounty-hunter. The Reaper shrugged, moved to the platform side and, gripping the rail, swung out so he could see the track ahead. "That grade the conductor was telling us about, it's coming up. We should be slowing any second." He moved back under the awning. "When we do," he said to Cary, "we jump."

The little man blanched. "Oh no."

"Oh yes," the Grim Reaper said with some emphasis. "You know me, Horatio. I got a way of insisting. Jumping ain't gonna hurt you, not if you do it right."

"It's not right to expect these things of me," the bank clerk whimpered. "I've never been an active man. You should know that by now."

"I also know you're learning," Grimm said, monitoring the train's pace.

"Don't be a bully," the old lady interjected; and the dog yapped again, displaying little sharp fangs under its curled upper lip.

"Don't interfere, lady," the Reaper said, "or the dog can test the jump for us!"

"Well!" she spluttered, cuddled the dog to her and looked in the opposite direction. "Freeloaders who haven't paid their fare, I'll be bound."

Grimm ignored her and carried on. "Now, all you gotta remember, Horatio, is let your legs go limp when you hit the ground. Then take as much of the impetus as you can by rolling."

A few minutes later the train noticeably slowed.

"Okay," Cary said, stepping backwards. "You go first and show me how it's done."

Grimm chuckled. "Nice try, Horatio. But you go first." He manoeuvred the apprehensive clerk to the steps.

"That way I can keep my eye on you."

Cary hesistantly felt his way down the iron rails until he was a few feet above the moving ground.

"You'd better jump of your own accord," Grimm said. "You'll only hurt yourself if I have to kick you off." He nudged the man as the train slowed a little more. Cary leapt away, crumpling as he made contact, and rolled down the grassy incline.

Grimm followed him down the steps, pushed off and hit the ground a couple of rods on. He winced with the pain star-bursting in his old joints as they took the brunt of the impact. The train was clanking its way some distance on when he hauled himself to his feet, still groaning at the effect of the fall on his body.

Judas Priest, he was getting too old for these games. He bent over and rubbed a rheumatic knee — and that's how come he didn't see the figure bearing down on him. He looked up just as the hand-pistol crashed down on his skull. The blow gave him more pain to think of, but only momentarily, for within a split second he was out cold, oblivious to all pains and aches.

Hammersley checked Grimm was unconscious, then loped back to the bank clerk, who had taken his custodian's instruction well and was now none the worse for his fall. Grimm had been right: he was learning. "You're in my custody now, Cary," Hammersley said. He indicated with a wave of his gun-barrel for his prisoner to move away at a right angle from the track. "I hope you've had a good rest on that train," the black-clad bounty-hunter went on, "because we're cutting across country. We're getting as far from the railroad as we can. I figure Jonathan decided to jump train at this point because of the possibility of a reception committee at the next depot. And I figure there's a big chance he was right."

13

SHERIFF Banner rode alone into the small railroad town. The men making up his posse had long since left him. As part-timers they all had jobs to do or spreads that needed tending back in Jefferson Springs and couldn't afford to waste any more time on a wild-goose chase. As they had kept reminding him, he was out of his jurisdictional territory. But he could feel his job slipping out of his fingers; and he was getting obsessional about the little bank clerk.

He passed the clapboard station building and reined in outside the marshal's office. The word on the sign that interested him was 'Federal'. Federal law knew no state and county boundaries. He tied his horse to the hitch-rail and took off his Confederate cap. He wiped his brow and slapped the dust from his hat before returning it to his head. Then he entered and made his presence known to Marshal Jed Langley. They were friends from way back.

"You're a long ways from home, Sam," the marshal said, taking a second tin mug to the coffee-pot on the stove. "What can I do for a fellow law officer besides giving him a cup of coffee?"

Banner took the cup and gratefully sipped at the scalding liquid. "There's a train due. By my figuring it's carrying a bounty-hunter escorting a prisoner name of Cary to Kansas. My interest is, Cary is wanted back in Jefferson Springs for absconding with funds from the lawyer's office there, where he was working."

"Know the name of the bounty?"

"Name of Grimm."

"Heard of him. Jonathan Grimm. Got quite a rep. The papers have tagged him the Grim Reaper." He finished his own coffee and wiped his lips. "Go on."

"As a town sheriff I can't legally take Cary now he's out of my bailiwick. You know that. But a federal marshal like yourself has the power."

"So you want me to arrest him?"

"Yeah. Then ride with him and me to the county line, where I can take over and ride him back to the Springs."

"A federal marshal can do that — sure. But what about Grimm? If he's the guy I'm thinking of, he's a determined hombre from what I've heard. He ain't likely to take kindly to the arrangement. It's a cert he'll aim to light out after you and reverse the deal once I'm off the scene."

"That's occurred to me too, Jed. But you could hold him for a spell on some charge. He's been like a burr under my saddle throughout this whole game. Give him some hoosegow hospitality. Just to give me enough time to get well on the way back to town."

"What's this Cary wanted for?"

"Walking out of the Pasco Mercantile Bank, Kansas way, with fifty thousand dollars."

Langley nodded. "Yeah. Now you mention it, I heard of that." He pointed to a collection of wanted-posters pinned to the wall. "Got a dodger on him." A likeness of Cary looked down from amongst the rogues' gallery. He rose, crossed the room and studied the picture more carefully. "Playing it strictly by the book, Sam, the Pasco job should have priority. But what the hell? Yeah, sure, I can help you. What are friends for?" He looked at the clock ticking loudly on the wall. "Train stops here for water. Due in about twenty minutes." He chuckled. "I don't like bounty-hunters anyways."

Its whistle-blast still bouncing over the flat terrain, the high-stacked locomotive grated to a standstill. The engineer swung himself down the iron steps of the driving-cab and made his way over to the raised water-tank.

Langley interrupted the conductor as he was walking to the station building. "You got a bounty-hunter with a prisoner on board?"

The old man stopped and looked the two lawmen up and down. "Don't know about that. There *was* a strange pair, but they weren't chained to each other, nothing like that. Not like you'd expect a bounty-hunter and his prisoner to look."

Langley looked at Banner then back at the conductor. "What car are they in?"

"They ain't. They jumped."

"God," Banner exclaimed. "Jumped?"

"Yeah. Sure is a puzzle why; their fares were paid."

"What did they look like?" Banner asked in agitation.

"One — tall, pale-faced feller. The other — on the short side."

"That's them," Banner said. "Probably guessed there'd be someone waiting here. That bounty's been hopping about like a wily toad from one means of

149

transport to another through this whole damn shindig."

"There's an old lady in the second car," the conductor went on. "She was on the observation platform at the rear when they made the jump. She saw it all. Maybe she can help you." He waved a hand at the train. "Be my guest. Now, if you'll excuse me, I got some paperwork to see to before we get steam up again."

The two men boarded the second car and made their way down the aisle. They found her with no problem and she confirmed what the conductor had said.

"Can you describe for us where they jumped, ma'am?" Langley asked.

"We'd just gone over a bridge. I remember that because it sounded rickety and I looked out of the window. My, it was a long way down." She hugged her dog closely. "Spencer doesn't like heights." Then she added, "Oh yes, the train was going up a grade when they actually jumped. I remember the tall man saying the train would slow and make it easier for them. Good job it did. The little man was plumb scared."

Langley looked at Banner. "The grade would be Sheep Pasture Pass. About a mile this side of the river." He touched his hat with a "Thank you, ma'am" before heavy-footing back down the aisle. "Come on, Sam. Let's go get 'em."

It was but a short while later that they saw Grimm hobbling along beside the track heading for town. "That's him," Banner said to his companion. "The bounty-hunter."

"Where's Cary?" he asked Grimm as the two riders reined in. His voice was hard with frustration. "The half-pint jerk get away from you?"

"With a little help from a guy called Hammersley," the Reaper grunted.

"Who's he?"

"Lee Hammersley. Another bounty-hunter."

"Hell, shoot!" Banner hissed through his teeth. "There's a helluva lot of fingers in this damn pie! Which way they head?"

Grimm waved vaguely north. "Ain't got a clue. The bastard pistol-whipped me before I knew what was what. When I came to they'd vamoosed."

"On horseback or walking?"

"It all happened so fast I couldn't see whether Hammersley had got horses.

"Ain't no point in going after 'em, Sam," Langley said.

"That mean you ain't coming for a look-see, Jed?" Banner asked.

"Hell, not knowing which direction they took, Sam, we could be sashaying around from hell to breakfast. There's a lot of prairie out there. You've notified that Cary's wanted for theft at Jefferson Springs, ain't you?"

"Yeah."

"Then it's best you get back to your office. There's nothing else you can do. Even on the slim chance of you catching up, you ain't got no jurisdiction. And I can't afford the time to ride with you."

"Least I can do," Banner said, pulling a rein to prepare his horse, "is see if I can pick up their trail as I ride past."

"Suit yourself, Sam," Langley said. "Meantimes I'll look after Mr Grimm." The bounty-hunter took the federal man's proffered hand and pulled himself up behind the saddle. He didn't see the wink the marshal gave the departing sheriff as they made their goodbyes; or he might have been suspicious of the helping hand.

14

IN town Grimm dropped from the marshal's horse. "Thanks for the ride."

"Don't give me thanks," Langley said, drawing his side-pistol. "Just give me your guns."

"What the hell?"

"You been giving the sheriff of Jefferson Springs some hassle on this caper. That constitutes obstructing the law and is gonna get you twenty-four hours in my slammer to cool your heels."

Grimm's hands hovered over his gun-handles.

"Go on," Langley said. "You could beat me, sure. But you'd be on the wanted-list yourself."

Grimm shrugged and allowed his guns to be taken. For a man who lived by guns he was sure spending a lotta time lately with empty holsters. "I probably couldn't catch Hammersley now anyways. He's a resourceful man and even if he's on foot, he'd get horses or some other transport mighty quick. Like you said, a body could be sashaying all over the goddamned place for weeks looking for 'em." He chuckled philosophically. "I need the rest anyways."

He wasn't lying when he said he'd take the opportunity to get a rest. The marshal's hospitality spread to coffee and a plate of beans, after which the bounty-hunter laid back on the bunk in his cell and fell instantly asleep.

He was flat on his back, stetson over his face when, much later, he was woken by voices. A couple of rough-and-ready cattlemen had brought a gun-shot man into town. After leaving him in the care of the doctor they had come to the marshal's office to report the affair.

"Found him on the trail," one was

saying. "Fair bleeding to death from a bullet wound in the leg. He'd been trying to walk but had collapsed. Anyways, we tourniqueted it and brung him in. Doc says much longer and he wouldn't have made it."

"How is he now?" Langley asked.

"Drowsy. But doc says he'll be okay. Huh, he won't he going no-place for a week or more."

"Any idea who shot him?"

"Well, that's one of the reasons we thought you might be interested, Jed. He was mumbling something about the Jesse James mob."

Jonathan Grimm shot up in his bunk when he heard the James name but before he could say anything the marshal had grabbed his hat and disappeared with the two cowpokes through the door on his way to question the injured man.

A quarter-hour later he was back. "Sure is a lotta folks interested in that Cary guy of yours," he shouted across to the cell. "The feller laid out on his back at the doc's is Hammersley, the guy you said bushwhacked you! Huh, the critter didn't get far before he got jumped hisself!" He explored the wanted-posters on his wall before selecting two and bringing them over. He held them up the other side of the bars for Grimm to see. "These two. Arch Clements and Dick Liddell. Two of the old James gang. That Hammersley guy's in the business. Says he's sure it's them. They ain't surfaced for a long time. Been holing up like the rest of the James outfit. I've telegraphed federal headquarters that they're in action again."

Grimm nodded. "Yeah. I know of 'em. About the only two left of the gang asides from Jesse and Frank and their cousins. Been lying low since Northfield." He shook his head as though he couldn't believe it. "So they've drygulched poor Lee and made off with Cary?" He pondered for a spell. "Pieces of the puzzle starting to fall into place."

"What do you mean?"

The bounty-hunter shook his head. "Oh no. The spot I'm in, I need an ace in the hole." He went back to his bunk, threw his legs up and leaned his back against the wall, thinking. Langley looked at him quizzically for a few moments then returned to his desk.

"Got a proposition, marshal," Grimm said later when the lawman brought him a coffee.

"What situation is a man behind bars in to make propositions?"

"As a federal officer, you'd be interested in Clements and Liddell, wouldn' you?"

"Sure."

"Well, I figure I know where they're heading."

"Where?"

"That's another ace to back up my first. The answer would be part of this proposition."

"I'm listening."

"Catching Clements and Liddell is federal business. You unlock this door now and I'll take you to where I figure they're heading. Then, if we have a showdown with 'em, you take the two James men and I reclaim Cary."

"Keep talking."

"Cary and I started to get on together. He's a harmless guy really. Not your run-of-the-mill owlhooter. Anyways, during one of our conversations, he named a place."

He told you where he hid the loot?"

"I think so. He didn't explain it that way. But it was important to him because he insisted on my repeating it so that I would remember it. At first I thought he was telling me where his folks were, so that I could report to them if things turned out bad for him. He was getting a mite worried about the way this scrape was shaping up rough. But I've been thinking about it. I figure it's where he's stashed the take. That's what the two James boys are after. The fifty thousand he heisted from the Pasco bank. Now, he gave me the information because we were beginning to get friendly, but they'll beat it out of him if he doesn't talk. He's only an ordinary feller and he won't stand up to much when they get nasty with him."

"You on the square about this deal?"

"Yeah. But from your angle you don't know, so you'd have to trust me."

Langley looked at the man in the cell while he thought. "You expect me to let you go without you telling me nothing?"

"Listen, we both know you got nothing on me. You're holding me for a little spite on Banner's part. Nothing more. Just doing my job, I've been getting in his way. That's all. Guys with a badge don't cotton to bounty-hunters. It's understandable. But I'm no more a lying criminal than you are, and you know it." He took a mouthful of coffee. "I'll tell you what. I'll give you *part* of my information in the interests of goodwill."

"Go on."

160

"Cary has stashed his take at Falls City. You heard of the place? Little town, just west of the Missouri."

"Is that it?"

"There's a bit more but I'm keeping that to myself till we get there. I gotta keep one good card against my chest."

Langley pondered some more.

"Clements and Liddell have been wanted a long time," Grimm said by way of encouragement. "Sure be a feather in the cap of the federal officer who takes 'em."

"Yeah," Langley said cynically. "And a helluva prize for the bounty-hunter who takes 'em in."

"True."

"Then why offer them to me? Why make do with a smaller bounty from the bank clerk if you're so sure about where Liddell and Clements are heading?"

"Because to stand a chance of getting any of the three I need to leave now. And the only way I can get out now is to offer you a carrot. And if that means you riding with me, so be it."

"So what's to stop you from reneging on our arrangement once you're clear of the bars?"

"Nothing, 'cepting my promise. Like I said, it's a matter of you having to trust me. No avoiding it."

Langley thought a spell more. Then he acceded. "Okay, Mr Bounty-Hunter, it's a deal."

15

THE further towards the east that Grimm and Langley travelled the more populated the region became. Farmers, miners, drifters, rivermen, traders. Along the trail they passed bright-eyed hopeful settlers setting out for the far west with their wagons weighed down with all their possessions. The two riders kept to the open trail for speed and to give themselves the best means of looking out for the three objects of their pursuit. Travelling by day, sleeping by night, they worked their way across the eastern region of the state, covering prairie and a virtually treeless landscape with belts of winter wheat interspersed with corn. Here and there in the more established part of Kansas, the one-crop system obstinately adhered to by the farmers for so many years was already leaving pockets of impoverished soil, portents of another possible future for Kansas, poverty through overworking the land. But then greener, wooded country as they moved closer to the land of the Missouri. Occasionally, in the distance, herds could be seen being driven up from all parts of the state, heading for the growing slaughtering and meat-packing plants of Kansas City.

Kansas, the state which had been dubbed *Bloody Kansas* being split down the middle during the Civil War, with half the population siding with the North and the other half joining the Southern forces. Where Kansas redlegs and Missouri jayhawkers had slaughtered each other. Where kith and kin had fought against one another. Where family rifts would last for generations.

It was on the fifth day near noon that the two near-exhausted horsemen finally rode into Falls City.

"Now what?" Langley asked as they swung their horses into what constituted the main street.

"Xanadu."

Langley leaned wearily in his saddle. "Is that it?"

"It's all I got, pardner."

"All this way on the strength of a word? Xanadu?"

"Yeah. That's all Cary said. Xanadu, Falls City."

"Jeez, Jonathan. Sounds like — hell knows what it sounds like. Something foreign. What does it mean?"

"Don't know."

"Well, how the hell do we use that nugget of information?"

"We ask questions."

They fixed a rendezvous at a saloon at the far end of the main street and split up to enquire about 'Xanadu'. Grimm tried a line of stores: general, animal feed, hardware retailers and, coming up with nothing, ensconced himself in the saloon and waited for his companion.

"I suppose I could rope in the local law," Langley said, finally dropping into a chair at the same table, having drawn a blank himself in his inquiries. "But I'm loth to do that. Five days on the trail has made this my pigeon now."

"*Our* pigeon, friend," Grimm grunted and ordered more drinks. "We got a bargain. Remember?"

There was some kind of trade convention in town and accommodation was not easy to find but eventually they fixed up sharing a room at an hotel. The younger of the two and with some energy remaining, Langley had immediately set off round the town again asking questions, but Grimm remained behind for a spell. His old body didn't take kindly to the accumulation of abuse it had been subjected to over the last weeks, including a five-day non-stop ride; and getting concussed by Hammersley's hand-pistol hadn't helped. Fatigue wasn't the word for it. As he kept thinking to himself: he was getting too old for this game. He needed one big bounty and it would be retirement. But that was ifs. Here and now he needed a spell relaxing. Promising his companion he would take up inquiries shortly he settled himself in a comfortable high-backed chair in the hotel lounge and lit up his pipe, intent on letting the world pass him by for a spell.

Nothing like a pipe of good tobacco. He leaned back, his eyelids drooping, only half aware of the comings and goings. It was in such circumstances that he overheard the blustering hotel proprietor in discussion with one of the cleaners.

"Can you come in tomorrow, Maisy? With the convention and all, the place is booked out and we're understaffed."

"I realize that, sir, but it's rather awkward. My time is spoke for all day tomorrow."

"Can't you change your schedule? I really need you."

"Well, tomorrow's the day we set aside for that Xanadu place."

"I was forgetting. Tell you what: I'll give you a bonus over your usual rate."

"I'll have a word with George."

Xanadu! The word suddenly assailed Grimm's consciousness and brought him back from his semi-dozing state. Xanadu: the way she was talking it sounded like a building. He heaved himself out of the chair just in time to see an elderly lady making for the door. Pulling himself together he followed her outside.

"Excuse me, ma'am," he said, catching her on the boardwalk. "Maisy, isn't it?"

The first thing she noticed was the stranger's disfiguring powder-burn on his cheek and she hesitated before saying, "Yes?"

"I hope you don't think it rude of me but I couldn't help overhearing your conversation just now. You said — the Xanadu place?"

"Yes, that's right. Xanadu." Her pronunciation of the word was a little different from Grimm's. "What of it?"

"Well, I need to visit there but I've been having trouble trying to locate it. Where would it be?"

The old lady looked him up and down, the suspicion in her eyes growing as she took in more of the trail-grimy, tired-faced old man.

Grimm chuckled. "I'm really not as bad as I look, ma'am. Been in the saddle for a long time, is all. Just rode in from the west and booked in at the hotel there with my friend."

"Well, can't see no wrong in telling you about it. It's public knowledge anyway. You'd have trouble if you asked for Xanadu because most people call it the Whitewinter place. After the family. Xanadu was old man Whitewinter's nickname for the place. The name of some grand palace he'd picked up out of the history books. He was a mite fanciful like that. Anyway, it's a large house about five miles out of town, sir. Got some acres of ground around it."

"Sounds a big one."

"Yes. It's a grand place. Used to belong to one of the richest families in these parts. The Whitewinters. Made their money from river business. You know, trading and such."

"There's a story behind it?"

"During the war there was some trouble. You know there were divided loyalties throughout the state at that time. The Whitewinter company was shipping arms up river for the South. Tried to keep it quiet and the old man claimed they were just honouring previous contracts. It's bad how some people make money out of war. Anyway, those in town siding with the North got to hear of it and, sir, they didn't like it. There was some rioting and some killing. The house was part burnt down. Nasty time that. It's been largely restored since though, of course. But the family have long since left. Too many bitter memories."

"What about now?"

"The place has had a succession of

owners since I don't know when. You say you're going there?"

"Yes."

"Well, you won't find anybody there. Not unless you've made some arrangements to meet somebody at the place. Nobody in occupancy. Been empty for years."

Might I ask, ma'am, what is your connection with the place?"

"There's a lawyer in town, handles real-estate. Anyway, acting on behalf of the owner, he pays us to tend to it. We go every two weeks. I clean the house. Just a matter of sweeping out the dust. While George, he's my husband, cuts the grass and keeps the weeds down."

Grimm pondered. A large empty house with acres of ground would be an ideal place for someone like Cary to stash loot.

"What's your interest? Are you thinking of buying it, sir?"

"No, just visiting. My friend and I, we've been asking around town but folks don't seem to have heard of it."

"Well, with the Whitewinters going so long ago and the house being empty and all, most folks will have just forgotten about the place. Not many remember the Xanadu name. Especially the younger ones."

"Five miles out of town, you say? Which direction?"

"On the north road. You can't miss it."

He touched his hat. "I'm beholden to you, ma'am."

The lady nodded and scuttled on her way, thinking "What a nice gentleman, after all."

As soon as Langley returned, Grimm was ready and waiting, informing him of his discovery. They agreed, despite their shared state of fatigue, that they would have to ride out there and then, but one look at their horses in the livery was enough for them to arrange rental of a couple of fresh mounts.

Even the short trip would be unfair on the critters.

"Sometimes there's an advantage in being a dumb animal," Grimm grunted wearily as he tested out the responses of his newly rented horse before nudging it out to the northern trail.

16

IF the original Xanadu had been the name of some fancy palace in history then it would have fitted the Whitewinter place in its heyday. It was one of those houses that Grimm associated with the Southern aristocracy. Large acreage with wooded sections, orchards and landscaped gardens, now somewhat overgrown, that once would have been the venue for wealthy folks' get-togethers, coming-out parties, birthday celebrations for young belles and beaux. And the building itself, even at the distance at which they first sighted it, could be seen to be aiming at grandeur with its ornately stepped entrance and mock classical facade, albeit in need of paint and renovation. A house old, inanimate, but still proud.

There was a long, fenced driveway

from the foreyard to the tall sentinel pillars marking the point where it met the trail. The two riders stopped a half-mile short of the formal entrance. The treeless prairie now far to their west, there was enough cover in the shape of foliage for them to pull in without being seen from the house.

"Reckon they're there yet?" Langley queried.

"Can't see anybody. But the place is too vast for us to be sure from here."

"Maybe they've been and gone. They had a start on us."

Grimm chuckled. "Nope. I've travelled with Cary. With him in tow they'll be lucky if they've kept any of their time advantage. Let's tie our horses hereabouts under cover. Away from the trail too, in case they're behind us. Then we'll make our approach on foot."

The two men split up and advanced at different angles. They hadn't gone very far when Grimm halted, raised a staying hand, then pointed. Langley stopped and looked in the indicated direction. There was movement some distance from the house. A man was digging with a shovel. Grimm recognized him. Weathered skin, lean, muscle-knots. A necklace of rings chinked from his neck as he worked. The two observers drew their hand-pistols and edged closer. There was another man, motionless, tied to the bole of a tree. Langley and Grimm watched silently without progressing any further. The observers were waiting for signs of a third man. They had a long wait but eventually they saw him, coming from around the other side of the main building, shovel in hand. The red, pockmarked face of Arch Clements. "Can't find nothing out there, Dick," the man shouted to his comrade.

Grimm worked his way sideways to get a better view of the tied man. He recognized him too: an unconscious Horatio Cary with a bloodied face.

The Reaper nodded his recognition to the lawman.

Liddell ceased his toil. "Hell! Get some water, Arch. We'll wake him up and ask the bozo again. This time we'll get the answer we want." The further man dropped his shovel and walked to a pump. After a few hand cranks he'd filled a pail. He picked it up, carried it over to the tree and emptied it over Cary. "I swear I'll kill the bastard," the other man said, oblivious of the signs now passing between the two hidden observers as they coordinated their silent approach.

"Hold it there and drop your weapons!" Langley bellowed moving quickly forward with Grimm following the same motion to form a pincer. "Federal marshal."

The men being challenged froze and turned. There was a swift exchange of glances, then both men moved fast. Clements, with the bucket and the nearer to Langley, threw it at the lawman with one hand, drawing his side-pistol with the other. Liddell pulled his gun on Grimm.

The two men, already holding their weapons, fired in the one instant. Langley's bullet scored the forearm of Clements' gun-hand while the bullet from Grimm's long-barrelled forty-four hit the chamber of the other man's gun so that a cartridge inside exploded. Liddell dropped it in pain and surprise.

"Don't try that again," Langley said. Two pairs of hands slowly rose skyward, Clements wincing from the wound in his arm, the blood from which was staining his shirt-sleeve.

"Well, well, well," Langley said. "What do you know? Archibald Clements and Richard Liddell. In person." He stepped forward, sheathing his gun. "Cover me, Jonathan, while I get the cuffs on 'em." He clicked them firstly onto Liddell who, unwounded, would be more of a threat, and then turned to the second outlaw who

178

was now gripping his reddening arm, standing near the prostrate Cary.

"Come on," Langley said. "It ain't all that bad." Clements swayed, moaning and groaning. Then, as Langley bent forward to fix the irons, the man rammed his knee in the lawman's groin, and grabbed his holstered gun as Langley doubled up in pain. Using the lawman as cover he raised the gun to fire at Grimm.

The bounty-hunter crouched but couldn't shoot because of Langley. Suddenly Cary's heel shot out, not hard but enough to unbalance the outlaw. Grimm leapt forward, pushed Langley clear and rammed his forty four hard into Clements' neck. "Drop it, you bastard."

Seconds later the lawman had composed himself and had the cuffs on him.

Langley rubbed his groin as he spoke to Grimm. "How many left of the James mob now?"

"Only a few, marshal. Jesse and

Frank. The Ford brothers. Maybe another."

Langley turned to the roughnecks. "You tell me where they're hiding out and it'll go easier on you. Especially the big fish, Jesse hisself. You give us his cover and we got some deal going."

The two men remained sullenly silent. He shrugged and fetched their horses. When he'd got them mounted, he turned to Grimm. "I'll leave you to finish off the Cary business as we agreed. Any problems with the Kansas authorities on the arrangements, refer 'em to me. I'll back you." He glanced at Cary. "He looks a bit of a mess but I reckon he's fit to take in and stand trial."

He put out his hand to the bounty-hunter. "We make a good team, pardner. If ever you've a mind for federal employment, you can look to me for a recommendation."

The Reaper sheathed his guns and took the hand. "Thanks, but another bounty or two under my belt and I'm gonna put myself out to pasture." Then he added with a chuckle, "I ain't as young as I look, you know."

Langley eyed the gaunt, creased features and grinned. "So long, pal."

Grimm watched him ride with his two charges down the splendid avenue, waved when he passed through the entrance onto the trail then knelt beside Cary who, with his lips puffed and bloodied, had not taken part in any of the conversation.

"How'd you get into this state?" Grimm asked as he untied him.

Cary opened his mouth to speak but hesitated with the soreness. He'd lost a tooth. He gingerly felt round his face before speaking. "When they put the pressure on me I gave them the same information as I gave you. Xanadu. Well, a little more. I gave them the Whitewinter name when they started hurting. But when we got here they started to get real mean and that got my goat. I thought — no, you bastards, treating me like that. I know you're gonna make me crack but I'm gonna hang out as long as I can."

He fingered his jaw. "And I did. I can be obstinate too. Didn't tell 'em nothing more. Huh, they been through the whole house. Tore up half the gardens."

Grimm looked around. He could see the signs. "Okay, smart-ass, where is it then? Where in the hell *did* you hide it?"

Cary chuckled. "Go on, you're an intelligent man. Guess."

Grimm looked around again and shrugged. "I'm tired, can't think straight. You don't wanna tell me, then don't. I'm too old and tuckered for any more games."

Cary raised his arms outward, wincing at the assortment of pain that the movement brought. "It's staring you in the face."

Grimm had given up. "I can't see it, you peckerhead."

Cary tried to laugh but it turned into a groan. "The property itself! I put the lot into buying the place in a false name. Now who's the peckerhead?"

Grimm chuckled.

"Then I went out to Jefferson Springs," Cary continued. "Took employment under the false name with Mr Eaton, the lawyer. My intention was to stay there until the heat was off, then come back here, sell up and move on."

"Ingenious. But why did you steal from Eaton? That was a chancy thing to do for someone trying to lie low."

"I know, but I got in a spot. The purchase of the Whitewinter place took virtually all that I had taken from the bank, and the lawyer in Falls City kept sending me new bills. For legal expenses and such. See, I left the deeds with him for safekeeping. At the time, naively, I thought even if I got arrested and did time I could always come out, sell off and still keep my loot. Maybe he smelled a rat, I don't know. Anyway, he started putting the squeeze on me, sending me unexpected bills, big ones. All looking genuine. You know, legal expenses and stuff. So, I thought I'd borrow from one bastard to pay off another. Never liked lawyers. Josh Eaton was a bit of a buffoon. I could easily have obscured the deficits for a spell, then returned the money when I'd come back here and liquidated my assets by selling the place. So I was only taking a loan really."

"Well," Grimm said, "I gotta thank you for saving me yet again. Kicking Arch Clements off balance like that when he got the drop on the marshal gave me my chance."

Cary shrugged but winced with the effort. Grimm watched him stagger painfully to his feet. "Come on, Horatio. I'm gonna get a doc to look you over."

17

THEY stood outside the doctor's surgery. Cary looked the worse for wear but he'd been cleaned up and, except being deficient by one in the tooth department, there was nothing serious.

"Come on, Grimm said. "Let's you and I partake of some good whiskey. We both need it."

"I don't take alcohol."

Grimm chuckled. "Is there anything you do — apart from robbing banks and lawyers? Come on, my treat."

The saloon was well patronized but they found a corner for themselves and Grimm introduced his companion to the pleasures of red-eye.

Cary spluttered on the drink then stared at the glass. "I been thinking. Everybody keeps talking about deals. I can offer you one."

The bounty-hunter had also been thinking. Kansas City wasn't far away now and he'd grown attached to the little pen-pusher. At least he'd have a go at things he wasn't used to. And he'd proved with Clements and Liddell that he'd got some guts under his threadbare waistcoat. The bounty-hunter was beginning to have second thoughts about taking in Horatio Cary after all. Just let the little runt scoot. A most un-businesslike action to take. But maybe there would be some reward in it for Grimm's revealing to the authorities about Xanadu and what form the bank-take was in. He'd been on the point of suggesting this to his little comrade when Cary played this card mentioning a deal. Okay, before he'd say anything, let him talk.

"Go on. But keep your voice down."

"I been pondering on why Clements and Liddell were so keen to get the loot from the Pasco bank. I listened to their conversation. They mentioned Jesse a few times. You know what? I think I inadvertently stole James gang money! Remember I told you way back there was one major account?"

"Yeah."

"I reckon the guy who opened the deposit was one of the James gang."

"Obviously he wouldn't use his real name. Can you recall the name he used?"

"Of course I can. I was the bank teller. I used to organize all the deposits and withdrawals. Somebody regularly putting in and taking out large amounts makes an impression. He didn't deposit the whole forty thousand in one go. Came in over a few months, putting it in piecemeal."

"One way to try to avoid suspicion. On the other hand, he could have been a genuine businessman."

"Of course he could. That's something that would have to be investigated. But the way things have turned out, I think not."

"Okay, what was the name?"

Cary chuckled. "My telling you that

would be the deal."

These thoughts had also crossed the Reaper's mind. "You know that depositor is likely to be none other than Jesse James himself?"

"Yes. And I've got more to bargain with. I remember the address of the depositor. Leastways, the town."

Grimm looked around at their fellow drinkers. Those that were in earshot were preoccupied with their own conversations. But one couldn't be too careful. "Listen," he said. "I've already got an hotel room booked in town. You and I will have one more drink, then we'll get over there, have a meal and talk some more."

In the quiet of the hotel bedroom, Grimm drew on his pipe, and reflected on the blue smoke wafting up to the high ceiling. Then he looked at the man lying on the bed. "Okay, Horatio. You give me what you know about this depositor. If it's Jesse James, you get your freedom, at least from me.

Cary raised his head, leant on his elbow and turned his beaten-up face to the bounty-hunter. There was a new glint in his eyes, the look of a man who had found something in himself he didn't know he'd got. An inner strength that had enabled him to take a hammering from hardened criminals and not yield. "Before we get around to that, what do I do in the meantime?"

"This guy lives some distance away?"

"A ride," Cary said, still keen not to give too much away.

"You can stay here while I investigate."

"What you gonna do? Chain me to the bedpost again?"

"No. I'm gonna have to trust you."

Cary nodded. "Very well. The man holds the deposit in the name of Howard. Thomas Howard. And when he came to the bank he came in a buggy, all respectable looking, from St Joseph."

"There must be plenty of banks in St Joseph. Why would he ride out to a small town?" Grimm drew on the pipe.

"I suppose he still had an inclination to obscure his trail, even when he had a false name. Wouldn't want people in St Joseph being nosey. This feller, what does he look like?"

"Black hair. Full beard. Very sombre appearance. You know, dark clothes. Looks like a businessman. Neat suit and waistcoat."

"That would be his cover for handling a large amount of cash." Grimm thought some more. He had a clincher and this was the time to drop it. "Anything else about his appearance? His face, for instance, apart from the beard?"

Cary shrugged. "Ordinary-looking, that's all."

Grimm didn't want to put words in Cary's mouth. The clincher had to come from him. He tamped down the tobacco in his pipe. "Anything about his eyes?" he prompted.

"Eyes? Oh yes, now you come to mention it. He blinked a lot. You know, a nervous twitch."

Grimm nodded. It was on record that Jesse James had an incessant flicker to his eyes. He'd been born with granulated eyelids and the discomfort caused continuous blinking. A nervous tic like that was something a man couldn't hide, because it would be so natural to him he wouldn't be aware of it. All the pointers were that Thomas Howard was the infamous outlaw.

"Horatio, I think we've hit pay-dirt. Anything else that might help?"

Cary swung his legs over and sat on the edge of the bed. "He's not alone. Sometimes he came in with a woman. Behaved like his wife."

"Oh yeah? What did she look like?"

"Comely-looking woman. Good clothes."

"You know her name?"

Cary pondered. "Can't recall. She didn't come in often and when she did, she didn't do any business at the counter. Stayed in the background."

Grimm rubbed his chin. "Well, there's enough to go on."

After a while Cary added, "He did speak to her in front of me once. I'm just trying to cast my mind back. When he first opened the account they came in together. There were two children too. Girl and boy. Then, when we'd finished the business, I escorted them to the door and opened it for her, the kids being a handful and all. He said something to her as they were leaving and it struck me at the time it was a rare name." He kept on thinking while the bounty-hunter fiddled with his pipe.

"All I can remember," Cary said after a spell, "was that it began with a Z."

Grimm raised his finger as the clue prompted his own brain. "Yes," he said after a while. "Zerelda. That's it. Same name as Jesse and Frank's ma. Strange name. It was a slip-up for him to use it in public like that. Well, that's a little bit more evidence." He knocked the dottle from his pipe. "I'd better start thinking about getting down there."

"Alone?"

"Yeah."

"Why don't I come? I can identify Howard."

"No. We don't know exactly where he is in St Joseph, and you'll spook him if he sees you first. Besides, this could turn nasty and you'd be in the way."

18

IT was the next morning when the Grim Reaper cleared flat, wooded country and found himself riding into St Joseph. It was a river-town with quays, wharfs and inlets. There were riverside hotels for folks desirous of a rest on their way north, the Missouri being navigable right up into Montana Territory and that was one helluva distance to cover in a boat. As he moved around he was aware of smells different to what he was used to: foreign goods being unloaded, fancy cooking, women with sophisticated perfumes. Near the river it was a hive of activity as, here and there, crates were winched up and heaved onto wagons, repairers worked on craft in their yards, riverboat captains bellowed orders. Away from the Missouri, the town itself showed the signs of associated prosperity: big buildings, business and bustle.

He was faced with his usual problem. He couldn't go around asking for this Mr Howard. That was going in with big feet; the news could get around and scare off whoever he was looking for. He toured the saloons, taking a long time over drinks, listening and looking. He read all signs as he passed. He bought the local newspaper and scanned it for any mention of a Mr Howard. By the afternoon he had got nowhere, but he was not perturbed. That was usual. Patience had always been the name of his game.

Time was not a problem. Howard wouldn't start to run if he didn't know someone was onto him. Grimm took a late lunch in a restaurant. Settling over a cup of coffee afterwards he opened his tobacco-pouch. Damn, nearly empty. During the past weeks he'd had other more important things on his mind than to think about re-stocking tobacco-pouches. He finished his drink quickly, paid the bill and stepped out into the afternoon sun. As he turned to walk along the boardwalk he collided with a passing man.

"Sorry, pal," Grimm said, angling his head to see the man's face. He was taken aback. He knew the face. It was the ginger-haired Samaritan who had picked him up off the prairie and taken him into Jefferson Springs when he had fallen off his horse all those weeks ago. "Well, I'll be . . . ," he started to say, shaking a forefinger as he tried to remember the name. "Hell, what a coincidence."

The man pulled a wry face, looked Grimm up and down, and shook his head. "You got me, friend. I don't know what coincidence you're talking about."

The young man made to move on but Grimm caught his arm. "Johnson. That was it. Bob Johnson out at Jefferson Springs. You remember me! The guy with a lump on his head. My horse got spooked by a sidewinder. You must remember! Hey, you did me one helluva favour. Shot a snake that was gonna put his grabbers into me. You recovered my horse, took me into town."

The man looked puzzled. "Jefferson Springs? Never been near the place, feller." He chuckled. "You're mixing me up with some other guy." He shrugged. "Sorry to disappoint you." He pulled himself free and moved away.

Grimm shook his head as the man proceeded across the road. "God damn!" he muttered to himself. "Sure is the spitting image." The likeness was so uncanny he wanted to ask if the man had a twin, but by then the fellow was far away attending to his own affairs.

Reluctantly he dismissed the matter and worked his way along the boardwalk until he came to a general store.

It was a large place, as one would have expected a store to be in a bustling metropolis like St Joseph. He was in luck. Rivermen, like their open sea brethren, were partial to their tobacco and the proprietor prided himself in catering to their needs in relation to the nicotine weed. There was a shelf of large jars, each containing some variety of pigtail, navy plug, shag and twist. Grimm was spoilt for choice and took some time before he made his selection while the understanding storekeeper looked on. Finally his customer opted for a quarter-pound each of three varieties.

"Very popular, this one, sir," he said as he weighed the first on his shiny brass scales. The place was rich in smells: tobacco, coffee, tea, spices, candy. Grimm noticed a section devoted to clothes and, while the man was fulfilling his order, he walked over and felt the material of a shirt. Too fancy for him, he needed something hard-wearing. But he sure needed another shirt or two, and some pants, his current wardrobe had taken a hammering over the last weeks; and, there and then, he set his mind to get some when the present operation was over. He was considering the price-tag on a set of longjohns when a young lad came from the back of the store.

"What are you doing, lad?" the proprietor asked, sliding some tobacco from the weighing-dish into a bag. "Have you finished off the orders yet?"

"Yes, sir," the pimply-faced youngster replied.

"Including Mrs Howard's?"

"Yes, sir. But I was just coming in to see if you wanted any help in here."

"As you can see, it's quiet. How many orders does that make now?"

"Four, sir."

The man looked at the clock. "Well, get the buckboard out and deliver them while there's still light by which to drive. You know I don't like orders hanging over until the next day."

With a "Yes, sir" the young man disappeared out back.

Mrs Howard! Howard was not an uncommon name. But there was a good chance . . .

Grimm quickly picked up his purchases, paid and hurried out of the store. He unhitched his horse as casually as possible and stood pretending to examine the harness until, minutes later, the young man came trundling down the alley on the buckboard. Grimm waited until he was some distance away, then mounted up and set his horse in slow, detached pursuit. Despite his youth, the lad could handle the wagon well, negotiating it through the town's traffic then up into wooded country.

The first house was a half-mile out of town. Some fifty yards back, Grimm pulled in under cover of a willow and watched. There was an old lady cleaning the windows and she turned from her task when the young lad called her as he jumped down. There was a jovial exchange of words as she moved to the gate and he heaved a box off the back of the buckboard. As he bore his burden up the path an old man in a wheelchair came to the front door to join in the banter. The whole brief episode was probably the high point in the invalid's day. The lad was soon on his way again and Grimm gigged his horse to continue shadowing the wagon. He noted where the house was, but put it at the back of his mind's index file. The place was unlikely to hold whom he was searching for.

The second domicile, further out along the river, looked more promising. A man in his thirties in dark clothes came to the door and took delivery furtively. There were no pleasantries, the transaction being as perfunctory as it could be. Even from his distant vantage-point the observer could make out the man had a black beard. But the bounty-hunter was still too far away to make out any nervous tics. This time Grimm lingered in the stand of trees once the lad had moved on. Then he nudged his horse forward at a walking gait so that he passed the house slowly in order that his ageing eyes could get a grip on the sign across the gate: the Reverend Oakley. Huh, a minister!

That explained the dark clothes — and removed another likelihood.

He nudged his horse into a trot to catch up with the wagon which was now out of sight. After a while he got a clear view of the trail ahead but there was still no wagon in view. It seemed like he'd lost the delivery-boy until he turned and caught a glimpse of him through a gap in wooded terrain way back to his rear cutting away from the trail. He turned and urged his horse into a gallop. Topping a rise, he was just in time to stop his mount from plunging down the other side noisily through bracken when he re-sighted the lad braking the wagon at a third house. It was a single-storeyed frame house, a substantial place on a small hill with a spread of ground around it. There were two children playing with a swing: a little girl sitting on it while a small boy pushed her. And a man in homespun shirt and denims chopping wood.

"Groceries, Mr Howard," the lad

shouted across the fence. Although Grimm was some distance away, the wind was with him and he caught the words. So that was Howard. Hadn't got the dark clothes on Cary had talked about. No matter. Grimm studied him keenly. You could tell a deal about a man by the way he moved. This Mr Howard swung the axe determinedly and capably. Unless he'd come up the hard way and kept in trim, he was no businessman. The man put down the axe and walked to the gate to receive the delivery. The step was that of a proud, determined man used to action.

Grimm waited until the boy had departed. No need to follow him any more. If this wasn't Jesse James it was certainly the Mr Howard who took deliveries from the general store. The bounty-hunter tied his horse to a low branch and leant against the tree, watching obscured by foliage. He was annoyed he hadn't got his binoculars, but they were wrapped up in his saddlebag at the ostler's where his beloved Andalusian was quartered. He reminded himself that it was a bad workman who blamed his tools and did his best to monitor the place with his ancient eyes. Howard carried the goods inside but didn't come out again. Grimm remained in his position for some time. He felt loth to go in brandishing a gun and shooting off his mouth unless he was sure this was James. There certainly was a similarity from what he remembered of the wanted-posters, but the requirement not to be seen himself had meant he hadn't been close enough to see details. The kind of detail he wanted to see to make confirmation was twitching eyes.

He was cautious. If he moved in and the man wasn't James, word could spread about the episode and spook the outlaw if he was in the vicinity.

He would sure like to have a look at James's poster to remind him of the man's features; but his roll of dodgers was in his saddlebag with everything else at the ostler's in Jefferson Springs. However, that particular deficiency could be remedied by going to the St Joseph law office and casting an eye over the notice-board. As the most wanted outlaw in the whole of the United States, James was big enough to have his features advertised in all law offices. It would be simple enough to get into the place on some pretext.

And while he was in town there were other questions he could ask. With the increasing probability that the wood-chopper down there was the outlaw and Grimm knowing where he was, he could afford to take the risk of being nosey. He unhitched his horse, swung into the saddle and headed back to town.

19

LEAVING his horse at a hitch-rail at the end of the street Jonathan Grimm made his way along the boardwalk until he came to the law office. The doors were fixed open and he went inside. St Joseph was like the eastern towns he had seen, inasmuch as its lawmen were dressed in blue uniforms and were called constables. A uniformed officer was seated at a high desk listening to a complaint by a member of the public. As the bounty-hunter had hoped there was a large notice-board in the foyer and he took the opportunity provided by the desk officer's preoccupation to investigate it. The wanted-posters were mixed in with an array of official-looking notices about ordinances and stuff. He glanced over them. Yes, there was Jesse James, without the beard. He was staring at it, absorbing the features, when the constable behind him asked, "And what can I do for you, sir?"

Grimm turned. "Afternoon, officer."

"Yes?" the man said, some sternness in his voice as he appraised the bounty-hunter who had all the look of a no-good drifter.

"I'm thinking about settling in St Joseph. Sure looks a nice town."

"It is. And we want it to stay that way. What's your work?"

"Put my hand to anything, sir."

"Well, it's a quiet place nowadays. If you got no ties, you'd do better for yourself moving up-river. With all them ore strikes they're a-getting at Alder Gulch it's boom times in Montana Territory. You can get up there by boat. The river's navigable as far as Fort Benton now."

Grimm nodded a "Thanks, officer" and left.

Outside he paused a moment on the boardwalk. He reckoned he would know if Mr Howard was James if he saw him close up, despite the beard. He returned to the general goods store.

"That tobacco I bought earlier is plumb good," he said to the proprietor. "Thought I'd purchase some more before I ride on through."

"We aim to please, sir. Which one would you like?"

Grimm gave his order. "I saw a guy in town today," he said as the storekeeper did his weighing, "I could have sworn it was an old buddy of mine. But I caught sight of him through a store window and when I got outside, I'd lost him in the crowd. Guy called Tom Howard. You don't know him, do you?"

"There is a Mr Howard in town."

"I knew it! That's probably him!"

"Couldn't wish to meet a nicer feller. And his wife."

"Yeah, I knew old Tom had got hitched. Two kids too."

The proprietor bagged the tobacco. "It must be him. Our Mr Howard has two children. Yeah, girl and boy. I'll tell you one thing. You were lucky to see your friend in town like that because he rarely comes in." He prided himself on knowing everybody in town and could tell his present customer was a stranger. "Like you," he went on, "he ain't what you'd call a local. Mind, he's been here some time."

"Hey, where's he live? I gotta look him up before I hit the trail."

"In a cabin north of town. The way he's settled in, looks like he's a-aiming to stay." He nodded to the window. "Quiet place we got here, you know. Not like it was when the Pony Express started from a-way up the street." Then he grunted in disdain. "But the expansion stopped when Kansas City was picked for the railroad. Kinda got bypassed by everybody and everything as a result. If it wasn't for the river, the place would be a ghost town now. Mind, there's a lotta traffic on the river nowadays. They've found out it's another way of getting through to Montana Territory and all the gold they're finding out there. Good luck to 'em! So, quiet place we got now. Mind, lotta folk prefer it that way. My business has nose-dived, but I make a living. That's all I want."

Grimm steered the conversation back to what interested him. "Talking about earning a living, what's young Tom do to earn his crust these days?"

"Now you come to mention it, I ain't seen him doing nothing. Not by way of employment. Quiet kinda guy. Some kind of businessman, I figure."

Yes, indeedy! If Mr Howard was James he was one helluva businessman! Out loud he said, "Yeah, that figures. He was a merchant when we were in close company.

The proprietor handed him the packet of tobacco. "Don't know what his business is now though. Who knows? Maybe hit pay-dirt and retired young."

"I'll have some of that chewing-tobacco while I'm here," Grimm interjected.

"He gets visitors from time to time," the storeman went on.

"Yeah?"

"In fact, come to think about it, there're two guys in town now that he's having some dealing with."

"Oh, yeah? I might know them too. We shared a lotta buddies. Broke a lotta bottles between us too!" Grimm pretended to get excited like some country hick. "Hey, we could have a swell get together if I know 'em. Who are they, where are they?"

"Don't know their names but they rode into town — ooh — must be three days ago." He handed across the additional packet. "All I know about them, they got a room in back of the eats house down the road a-piece."

Grimm chinked some coins on the counter. "I've got a little time in town before I move on. I'd love the chance to see Tom again. Now, don't you tell any of them about our little chat. I'd like to surprise 'em. Boy, will we celebrate! I just hope there's enough booze in town to accommodate us!"

The proprietor tilled the money and took out some coins.

Grimm winked. "No, keep the change."

The man smiled and nodded as Grimm touched his lips with a finger in the universal gesture of silence. The bounty-hunter stepped out into the late afternoon sun. He took a bite of tobacco and leant against an awning support while he pondered. He moved the wad slowly around his mouth, spreading the flavour, while he looked the place over and pin-pointed the eats house. Towards the more sleazy part of town.

He strolled casually down the sidewalk, eyes on the building, a loose-planking shack, that might not even have had the fortune to see better days. No activity save for the wisp of smoke coming from the centre chimney-stack.

He walked down the alley at the side

to check the rear. Three horses. The owner's and the two James visitors?

He returned to the front and pushed open the door. A greasy smell hit him. He'd smelt worse; and he'd got hungry spending the afternoon learning the geography of the place during his time following the delivery-wagon. He ordered a steak and sat near the window so that he could cover the street as well as the middle door which opened onto the eating-room. From the noises behind the partitioning he knew there were at least two men in the obscured rented quarters.

There were no developments until the bounty-hunter was getting towards the end of the hunk of leather that had been served as steak. The door from the living-quarters opened and a man came out. He was well-scrubbed and neatly dressed. Short jacket, no guns. But Grimm caught enough of the face as it passed to link it to a name — Charley Ford, one of the old James gang! He'd seen that on a few posters. That really was the kicker. It would be too much of a coincidence for Jesse and at least one of his erstwhile henchmen to be in a town at the same time without there being design in it. His mental eye roamed over the family tree as best as he could remember it: cousin to Jesse, had a brother, Bob. The brother was probably the one remaining out of sight in the other room.

The man returned minutes later, he guessed only having been out to buy some small item from a store. There was the same lack of urgency to his behaviour as there had been to that of the man he figured to be Jesse. It was manifest they were all confident as to their remaining undetected. Not unjustifiably. It had been over a year since they'd been seen or known to be involved in criminal activities. They had realized that even for owlhooters of the stature of the James gang, the heat must wane with time.

Jonathan Grimm pondered on his next move. He could take them now. Would be no problem. They weren't expecting trouble. If Charley didn't carry guns to avoid suspicion, it was likely Bob didn't either. No doubt they had weapons hidden away in their room but he could handle it. But that wasn't the way. They would only pull in chicken-feed compared with the big money on Jesse. The ruckus that would be created by Grimm's apprehending the Fords would easily get back to Jesse and warn him. Besides, once he'd got Jesse there was the distinct possibility he could pull in the Fords as a bonus. No, here and now, best to get the lie of the land before initiating any action.

Again he felt irritated that the tools of his trade were with his stored saddlebags. He needed to watch the James house for a spell before acting and he could sure do with his old binoculars again. He returned to the main street and found a chandler's stores from whence he bought an eyeglass. Then, in the solitude of an hotel bedroom he cleaned his forty-fours before turning in for the night.

20

I T was the next day: the third of April. The year: 1882.

Jonathan Grimm rose early and rode out to the James house. He dismounted and, leaving his horse hitched well out of sight to the rear, circled the building at a distance. Settling down behind a spruce he focused the newly-purchased eyeglass on the window of the cabin. Except for stirring his ancient joints occasionally so they wouldn't go rigid on him, he hardly moved for an hour. No point in rushing.

During that time the man with the beard had come outside twice and Grimm had got a good view of his features. Even from a distance, through the glass the eye-twitch was very plain. No mistake, this was the most famous — or infamous — of the James brothers. Certainly he was playing the part of the respectable family man, like he was born to it. The flower and vegetable gardens had all the signs of being attended daily.

What was the point of all this? What had the great Jesse James been doing with his time before his funds were stolen from the Pasco bank? Waiting for something? For what? Biding his time? Why? Or was this a legitimate attempt to settle down, to lead an ordinary life in obscurity?

The tallow-faced hunter compressed his spyglass and pushed it into a saddle bag at his side. It was not for him to reason the whys and wherefores. The simpler his part in the judicial system the better. He worked his way back, threw his saddle bag over the back of his horse, and re-tethered the animal for fresh grazing.

"You stay here, boy. Rest nice and easy. While the old man goes off to earn the hay!" He glanced at his pocket-watch before moving.

Just before eight o'clock.

There was a pine-filled crevice descending to the flat land before the rise to the house. He inched down under cover of the trees. Damn! Riders were coming. He lay back against bark and peered through foliage. Two men. Could be the Ford brothers. They hitched their mounts outside the cabin, knocked at the door, entering without waiting for permission. Had to be someone close to behave like that. Must be the Fords.

He waited, saw the woman come from the kitchen, then return. He loped down the grade and up across the clearing that surrounded the house, and proned himself against the outer wall in between the door and window. The voices were quite distinct.

"When's his majesty getting his ass outta bed, Zerelda?"

"He's risen all right," she said, "but he's having a wash to freshen up. Been awake most of the night. He was up late doing some thinking, then couldn't sleep. Seems to have something on his mind."

Then she shouted. "Dingus!"

Grimm knew that to be Jesse's name within the family. "Remember," she continued, "it was you who asked your cousins to come early."

A muffled answer.

"I'll get you some coffee." After the woman had gone to the kitchen there was the sound of bare children's feet. "Hi, Uncle Bob."

"Hello, Mary. Hey, that's squeezing the life out of me."

The bounty-hunter could hear some horsing around.

Hello, Uncle Charley."

That was the second name. He had been right as to the identity of the two men staying in town. The same two who had come calling early in the morning. Bob and Charley Ford.

More horseplay. "Tarnation, you're gonna be a real strong man when you grow up, Jesse." That Jesse was the boy named after the father.

Grimm didn't like the notion of kids around when he made his move.

More sounds of play, then heavy feet. "Hell, you're early, boys!"

It was another voice. Deep. That would be the elder Jesse. "I didn't reckon you to be this early. When I asked you to come this morning I didn't expect you with the lark!"

Bad news, Dingus."

That's enough, kids. Your uncles and me are gonna have a talk. So, scat!"

Feet, door closing.

Grimm felt better with the children gone.

"Bad news?" James asked. "What?"

"The feds have got Arch and Dick."

"When, where?"

"Dunno. We got the news last night."

"God, the net's closing. They don't give nobody a chance.

There was a pause before the outlaw continued. "Then we ain't gonna get that bank money back."

"I did my best but I lost track of the runt the other side of Jefferson Springs."

"I know you did your best. But the fact of the matter is I'm skint."

"Us too."

"Ever since you first came back empty-handed I been facing up to the fact that that money ain't gonna turn up. Even if Arch and Dick got the money, I don't know whether we would see it. That's why I was developing an idea last night."

"What's that?"

"We lose our bank money, so we take somebody else's. The Platte City Bank. I been doing some investigating. This is the day in the month when deposits are at their highest. I've put a plan together for a raid tonight."

"God, not another one, Dingus. We're all too hot!"

"It's been a year since we pulled anything. This one's a cinch."

"They're never a cinch. Those days are over. None of us are getting any younger. Christ, this is never gonna end until we're all dead." There was a pause before Bob Ford continued. "Listen, you tried to work a stake in California with Frank, Charley and me but some bozo started to get suspicious and we had to lam it. California, Tennessee, Colorado, you've not been able to stay in any one of 'em."

There was a long pause, then Jesse's voice. "What are you suggesting?"

"You're living in a fool's paradise, Dingus. You think you're gonna find peace. But this ain't gonna last. It'll all catch up with you. Next week, next year. Sometime, for sure."

Sooner than that, brother, Jonathan Grimm thought.

"And what do you offer as an alternative?" This voice must be Jesse's, he surmised. "Giving ourselves up! You believe all that crud the state governor's dishing out about leniency if any gang-member surrenders? Bob, I'll tell you what leniency means. Life imprisonment instead of hanging. What good's that? Or ten years — off a hundred!"

"He'll keep his word, Dingus. He's gotta. He's made the offer public."

"He'll keep his word all right — but to the letter. Look at it realistically. It's more than his job's worth to give us much. What do you think it'll do to his re-election chances if he's on record for being soft on us? The most wanted men in Kansas and Missouri!" That last syllable came out as a flat 'a' in the custom of the local-raised.

There was the noise of children again. God, Grimm didn't cotton to that.

"Get them damn kids back into the kitchen, woman. I've told you they're not to be around when me and the boys are talking business."

The noise of children being unwillingly ushered from the room could be heard. A door slamming, then quiet. Grimm put his hand on his gun-handles.

"Anyways, you and Charley have been in contact with that governor too much to my way of thinking," James said.

"What's that supposed to mean, Dingus?"

"Smells like double-crossing on me, that's what."

That ain't fair, Dingus, and you knows it. If you don't cotton to taking advantage of the governor's offer and we give ourselves in, you know we won't say anything about you and your where-at. Landsakes, Dingus, we're kin."

James's voice took on an ominous tone. "And you know what would happen if you did spill on me. If I didn't get you, Frank would."

There was silence for a while. Then, "Well, if that's your last word, Dingus . . . "

Grimm had heard enough. Not only was it likely that the two men would be heading for the door, but if they came quiet there'd be debate over the reward

225

on them. And the kids were out of the room.

He squared up to the door, forty-fours out. Arching his leg, he simultaneously kicked the door and thumbed his guns.

21

THERE was a crash, splintering, and Jonathan Grimm was in the parlour, legs apart, his big Colts levelled.

"What the . . . ?" Jesse James shouted. None of the three men carried guns.

"Parley's over, boys," Grimm stated firmly, his gun-barrels positioned to nip any untoward action in the bud. "I'm taking you in. All of you . . . "

He faltered. If he'd done so with three armed men standing before him he would have been in trouble. But his sudden irresolution was instinctive — the result of shock. One of the three men was already personally known to him — as Bob Johnson!

"You're . . . Bob Ford?" he spluttered, staring at the familiar features topped with ginger hair.

x

227

"Yeah. Small world, ain't it?"

Jonathan Grimm quickly regained his composure as his eyes met the fluttering eyes of the world's most famous outlaw.

"It ain't ending as easy as this, cowboy," Jesse James said firmly.

The Reaper concentrated on James, capitulation being writ large over the faces of the other two.

"You've had a good run," Grimm countered. "And you know all good things must come to an end."

Both Bob's and Charley's hands were up.

"Okay, take us in," Bob said quietly. "I'm glad it's all eventually over."

Grimm side-stepped to give access to the outside door. As he moved James turned and leapt back. His hands were on the frame of a picture on the wall. Grimm fired out of instinct. A red blotch starred the shirt on Jesse's back. The hands clawed at the picture and he collapsed.

"Judas Priest," Grimm mouthed.

There was a scream from the side of the room as Mrs James burst in.

"Get her outta here," Grimm snapped, leaping forward to the fallen man. No need for a doctor to certify death. He'd seen it too many times to need confirmation. It had been a central, killing shot. Jesse James was dead.

The man known as the Grim Reaper lifted the picture from the wall, revealing a gun suspended by supports in a specially made recess. "I thought there was something odd about the way that picture was a-hanging when I came in," he grunted, extracting the gun and pushing it into his belt.

"Yeah," the other said. "In his new, law-abiding role Dingus didn't like any guns visible."

"We don't want his kids seeing him like this," Grimm said. He glanced around the room. There was a thick crocheted blanket draped over the back of the settee. He used it to cover the body.

Only Bob Ford was left in the room, his brother having gone to pacify the new widow in the kitchen. "Can I trust him out there?" the tall man queried, indicating the closed door with his re-cocked gun.

"I can't speak for Zerelda," Bob Ford said. "She's a passionate woman and she's just lost her husband. You'll need to keep an eye open. If she can find a gun I don't know what she might do. Over there in the chest, you'll find Dingus's working-guns.

Grimm backed over and lifted the lid of the chest. Rummaging underneath a pile of neatly-folded blankets he found a belt with two holstered guns. He draped it across his shoulder.

"I don't think there are any other guns in the place," Ford said. He dropped onto the settee, his head in his hands. "Don't be concerned about me and Charley. We ain't got no more running left in us. Our nerves have been near to breaking-point for a long time. Four states we been hiding out in. Had to keep moving. Neither of us could take much more. Always looking over your shoulder. That's no life."

He looked down at the still form of his cousin. "Dingus was stronger than us in that respect." He sighed. "It ain't surprising that it should end this way. He wouldn't believe that the governor would be lenient. Said there had to be a trap there somewhere."

Grimm went to the kitchen door, opened it a fraction. He could see Charley Ford was doing a good job in calming the woman down. The perplexed children were leaning against her, a look in their innocent eyes that the bounty-hunter didn't like to see. He closed the door quietly and looked back at the ginger-haired man. "What were you doing out at Jefferson Springs when you found me thrown from my horse?"

"Huh. On top of all our other troubles, Dingus had put a heap of money in the Pasco Mercantile Bank and it got robbed. Poetic justice, some would say. You might not have heard of that job."

Grimm chuckled. "I heard of it."

"Anyway," Ford went on, "the bank was having to shut down as a result, which meant he wouldn't get any of it back. It was all we'd got between us. Anyway, I got word the guy who did the heist was heading out that way. We all had a stake in that money so we all went a-looking. Arch and Dick went one way, me another. I didn't find the pecker though."

The tall man sniffed. "From what I heard of the conversation, you've had communications with the governor?"

Ford looked sheepish. "Yeah."

"You didn't tell Jesse, but I figure the governor offered you a reward if you brought him in?"

"Sure. Ten thousand bucks. Same as anyone else could have earned. He told me and Charley if either of us were forced into killing Dingus while attempting his capture he would pardon us after going through the formalities of a trial. But I couldn't do it. That's another thing Dingus wouldn't believe. Thought I could sell him out. Sure, I could have used the money. Who couldn't? But, like I told him, we were kin."

Jonathan Grimm pondered. Then, "How'd you feel about gaining a reputation as a man who shoots in the back?"

"I don't understand."

"Well, in the last thirty seconds I've rapidly adjusted to the fact that I've ended up on a bum steer in this caper."

"How's that?"

Jonathan Grimm returned his guns to leather. "You saved my life some time back. I can't take you in, not after the way you helped me. Now, the way the talk was going before I bust in, Charley was ready to give himself up with you. I couldn't sling a rope around his neck and drag him in either, him being your brother and all."

"You'll be paid for doing for Dingus. He was wanted dead or alive."

"Huh," Grimm grunted. "That's the rub. I been many things in my life, but one thing I ain't and that's a back-shooter. And I ain't aiming to start now. A guy has to have some principles. Sometimes even if he can't afford them." He pulled back the crocheted blanket and nodded at the blood on Jesse's back. "The way that bullet hit him, that was an accident. It happened so fast. I didn't intend it that way. The circumstances . . . "

"So?"

"The way I see it — you and Charley hand yourselves in like you were gonna. Strike the best bargain you can with the governor. Take in Jesse at the same time. Say it was you that did it. That should influence the governor in deciding punishment — and you claim on Jesse at the same time. I won't say anything. I'm washing my hands of the whole shebang. It's soured up on me.

You're all family. I figure you'll see to the looking after of Mrs James and the kids. With the ten grand, you'll have the dough to do it." He chuckled without humour. "What's more, if you don't mind circuses, I figure there's a fortune to be made at shows as 'the man who shot Jesse James'. Wild West shows pull big money back east."

Bob Ford shrugged. "After all I done over the years with the gang, I ain't concerned about folks pegging me as a back-shooter." Lines of puzzlement suddenly creased his forehead. "But I don't get it. Seems like bounty-hunting is your trade and you're losing a fee. Are you sure that's the way you want it to be?"

Jonathan Grimm patted Bob Ford's shoulder and then put a hand on the door handle. "Like I said way back — I owe you one."

He went outside. "See to things. And tell Mrs James that what happened wasn't the way I intended it turning out. I know it won't be much comfort to her but it'll make me feel a little better."

He didn't say goodbye, just moved slowly down the hill to his waiting horse. Principles sure come expensive, he mused.

22

"SO you're free to go," Grimm said when he'd finished telling Cary the story back in Falls City.

"But, letting Bob Ford take him in and claim the bounty, you're getting nothing out of Jesse James's being brought to book."

"That's the way it's turning out," Grimm said, a chuckle and a tired sigh of resignation mixed up in his voice. "But you and I had a bargain, Horatio. You were right about Howard being James. And you kept your part of the deal by staying here until I returned. It was my decision not to make capital out of it. Ain't no fault of yours."

"Anyway, I've been thinking a lot while you've been away, Mr Grimm. I've learnt a lot of things in the last weeks. I couldn't take a life being on the wanted-list. Always suspicious of strangers. Waiting for someone like you to track me down."

Grimm laughed. "You're not Jesse James, you know. You ain't gonna be chased very far. If you write to the Pasco bank and tell them that the stolen money is all bound up in the Whitewinter house, they'll get their lawyers onto clearing liquidation of the asset. Okay, the law will still want you. Yes, ain't no denying. But the heat will be off."

"I still don't want to be in that position."

"Listen, you bozo. They ain't gonna put much effort into trying to trace you. You'll be bottom priority, confined to the bottom of the pile. If you're still worried, move east. There's lots of banks in New York. And I don't mean for knocking over! I mean for getting a straight job. That's the work you like and can do. Nobody'd ever find you there; be like looking for a needle in a haystack."

"No. There's more to it than that. Like you say, I'm no Jesse James. One of the ways I'm different is I've got a conscience. It's been bugging the hell out of me ever since I did the job. It still is and will keep on bugging me till I've given myself up. That's the way I'm built; a bag of nerves."

Grimm shook his head. Judas Priest, there was no talking practicalities into some people.

"Hell, Horatio. Sleep on it."

He did and the next morning he insisted on Grimm taking him in and claiming the bounty on him.

Jonathan Grimm pushed through the front door of an hotel. It was four months later in a small town partway into the timber country of the Ouachita Mountains, Arkansas. The place was more of a lumber-camp than a town, with warehouses, planing-mills and stacks of raw lumber. The smell of fresh wood permeated the whole place, even the hotel.

Hearing about the new campaign at Fort Smith initiated by Hanging Judge Isaac Parker, Grimm had worked his way south to Arkansas. They were solid on law there, with the judge setting up this operation to wipe out the legion of owlhoots who infested the Indian held lands. Even though the U.S. Marshal's force had been supplemented by two hundred officers, they were still happy to use extra help and when he'd offered his services they'd pin-pointed the likely location of two hardcases for him.

The hotel was the only one in town but it ran to two storeys. There was a girl behind the reception desk. "Yes, sir?"

"Tell the two upstairs they've got a visitor."

"Which two, sir?"

"You've only got two staying here." He knew that much because he'd been watching the place before making his move.

"Oh, those two," she said innocently.

"Who shall I say is calling?"

"Tell them Jonathan Grimm's down here and wants to see them."

"Right away, sir." The girl moved quickly from around the desk and disappeared clip-clop up the stairs. At the end of the corridor, she threw open a door. One man was peering into an angled mirror, shaving over a large basin of water. The other, all ready for a good night out in the lumbermen's saloon, was lying on the bed waiting for his friend to finish.

"Can't you knock, woman?" the one on the bed snapped.

She closed the door quietly behind her and whispered, "There's a man downstairs asking for you two."

"He got a name?"

"Jonathan Grimm."

"He look like law?"

"No."

"Hey," the shaver said, wiping his unfinished face, "I heard of him. He must be working with Judge Parker. He's worse than law! Let's git!"

241

Minutes later they were out through the window and onto the roof of a lean-to. They slithered down the shingles and dropped to the ground. As one landed a figure came from under the lean-to and clubbed him with a pistol-butt on the back of the neck. The second one landed but his legs were kicked from under him and he sprawled on his face. He jumped up and found himself looking down the wrong end of Jonathan Grimm's forty-fours.

"Never fails," the bounty-hunter said wearily. "Even in Arkansas." He circled and backed away so that he could check that the one on the ground was still out. "Drop your gunbelt," he said to the one standing. "One hand. Left. Keep your other hand high."

The man fumbled with the buckle until the whole belt dropped.

"Now," Grimm said. "We gonna be sensible?"

"Sure," the man stuttered. "I wanna keep my head on."

Grimm appraised him and made a judgement. I'll buy that." He sheathed his guns and released the handcuffs hanging in readiness from his own belt as he walked slowly towards the man.

"Lenny!" a voice suddenly shouted to his side. It was the girl from the front desk throwing a six-shooter. Then, as Grimm was distracted, the fallen man came to, quickly assessed the situation and pulled his own gun.

The bounty-hunter's guns were in his hands and exploding at right angles to each other. One bullet took the standing man clean in the heart, giving the impression it had impaled him to the post of the lean-to. The bullet from the other gun channelled through the prone man's ribs and lungs.

Grimm exhaled noisily. He hadn't wanted it to end this way. He was good, yes, but he couldn't see around corners. He kept his long-barrelled forty-fours still levelled and cocked until he was sure.

Then he was sure and the weapons

slipped back into leather. He was two days riding back to Fort Smith, with the two men slumped over their horses in tow behind him. During the long trek there was a heap of time for thinking.

He thought about the James incident. That escapade had been four long months ago. Bob Ford had surrendered and had been tried for the murder of Jesse James. He had been convicted and immediately been pardoned by the governor. After the death of the outlaw, Jesse James's gunbelt and guns had been auctioned off for the grand sum of fifteen dollars. Now, even as far south as Arkansas, he was beginning to hear tales of Jesse's mother selling a whole stream of guns that she sincerely guaranteed to be the genuine possessions of her late son. And the last thing Grimm had heard about the Ford brothers was they'd started to tour the music-halls with an act called 'The Outlaws of Missouri'. *C'est la vie.*

Then he thought about Horatio Cary.

The two thousand he'd got for the pen-pusher was a fraction of what he would have had for taking in Jesse James. There are times when you can't win all the marbles.

However, the judge adjudicating on the case had taken account of Cary coming clean on what he had done with the embezzled funds; and also of his identifying Howard as James so that that portion of the James loot could be recovered. Grimm had taken time off to speak for him — Hell knows why, because he had his own living to make — but he did so, testifying that Cary had given himself up willingly and had given no trouble in being taken in. The net result: the judge lobbed his sentence down to three months.

Grimm had supplied six hundred dollars and got Cary, before the start of his short prison-term, to send it to Eaton at Jefferson Springs with a message that he'd only intended taking the lawyer's five hundred as a loan and it was being returned herewith

with interest. Eaton was a squaredealer and had dropped the charges. The last thing Grimm had heard was the little pen-pusher was out of prison, had returned to Jefferson Springs, and he and Mrs van Damm were planning to get married.

And good luck to 'em, he thought. Coming out of timber country with his grisly freight in tow he met the Arkansas River gushing down from Colorado and he nudged the Andalusian to follow it into Fort Smith.

Fort Smith was a big town with houses made of stone. The 'high sheriff', for such was how they called the head guy in the Fort Smith law office, authorized payment of five hundred dollars each for the two stiff hardcases he took in. A thousand dollars, and it had taken four weeks to track the bozos down. At least, a few more marbles in the bag.

Hell, he could do with a drink. One thing, Fort Smith wasn't short on saloons, and he entered the first one he came to after he'd got his money. The air was thick with smoke, the bar jammed with men each staking a claim to his eighteen inches of polished wood and foot-rail. There was little room at the tables where men were drinking and playing cards. A few were listening to the buckskin-clad troubadour on the small stage in a corner, strumming a guitar and wailing a mournful ballad.

Grimm bought a half bottle of rye, more to commiserate with himself on the poor bounties than to celebrate. The big ones were getting few and far between these days, now the heyday of the likes of the James, Daltons and Youngers were gone. The trouble was the law was moving west faster than you could say lickerty-split; less need for dollar-hunters to fill in the cracks. But it was still a living.

A drinker sitting next to him tried to strike up a conversation but, just for the moment, the gaunt-faced stranger wasn't interested in talk. He was more concerned with the song. His steel-blue eyes became slits as he focused on the singer. The song was a new one but he knew it was fast becoming popular because he'd caught snatches of it in saloons before.

But it intrigued him and he wanted to listen because he'd never heard the lyrics all the way through.

It was called 'The Ballad of Jesse James' and was about a guy called Bob Ford. The bounty-hunter turned his head so his old ears could catch all the words. When he heard the last lines:

" . . . and the dirty little coward,

who shot Mr Howard,

laid poor Jesse in his grave."

Jonathan Grimm smiled grimly to himself and emptied his glass.

Other titles in the Linford Western Library:

TOP HAND
Wade Everett

The Broken T was big. But no ranch is big enough to let a man hide from himself.

GUN WOLVES OF LOBO BASIN
Lee Floren

The Feud was a blood debt. When Smoke Talbot found the outlaws who gunned down his folks he aimed to nail their hide to the barn door.

SHOTGUN SHARKEY
Marshall Grover

The westbound coach carrying the indomitable Larry and Stretch headed for a shooting showdown.

FIGHTING RAMROD
Charles N. Heckelmann

Most men would have cut their losses, but Frazer counted the bullets in his guns and said he'd soak the range in blood before he'd give up another inch of what was his.

LONE GUN
Eric Allen

Smoke Blackbird had been away too long. The Lequires had seized the Blackbird farm, forcing the Indians and settlers off, and no one seemed willing to fight! He had to fight alone.

THE THIRD RIDER
Barry Cord

Mel Rawlins wasn't going to let anything stand in his way. His father was murdered, his two brothers gone. Now Mel rode for vengeance.

ARIZONA DRIFTERS
W. C. Tuttle

When drifting Dutton and Lonnie Steelman decide to become partners they find that they have a common enemy in the formidable Thurston brothers.

TOMBSTONE
Matt Braun

Wells Fargo paid Luke Starbuck to outgun the silver-thieving stagecoach gang at Tombstone. Before long Luke can see the only thing bearing fruit in this eldorado will be the gallows tree.

HIGH BORDER RIDERS
Lee Floren

Buckshot McKee and Tortilla Joe cut the trail of a border tough who was running Mexican beef into Texas. They stopped the smuggler in his tracks.

BRETT RANDALL, GAMBLER
E. B. Mann

Larry Day had the choice of running away from the law or of assuming a dead man's place. No matter what he decided he was bound to end up dead.

THE GUNSHARP
William R. Cox

The Eggerleys weren't very smart. They trained their sights on Will Carney and Arizona's biggest blood bath began.

THE DEPUTY OF SAN RIANO
Lawrence A. Keating and
Al. P. Nelson

When a man fell dead from his horse, Ed Grant was spotted riding away from the scene. The deputy sheriff rode out after him and came up against everything from gunfire to dynamite.

FARGO: MASSACRE RIVER
John Benteen

The ambushers up ahead had now blocked the road. Fargo's convoy was a jumble, a perfect target for the insurgents' weapons!

SUNDANCE: DEATH IN THE LAVA
John Benteen

The Modoc's captured the wagon train and its cargo of gold. But now the halfbreed they called Sundance was going after it . . .

HARSH RECKONING
Phil Ketchum

Five years of keeping himself alive in a brutal prison had made Brand tough and careless about who he gunned down . . .

FARGO: PANAMA GOLD
John Benteen

With foreign money behind him, Buckner was going to destroy the Panama Canal before it could be completed. Fargo's job was to stop Buckner.

FARGO:
THE SHARPSHOOTERS
John Benteen

The Canfield clan, thirty strong were raising hell in Texas. Fargo was tough enough to hold his own against the whole clan.

PISTOL LAW
Paul Evan Lehman

Lance Jones came back to Mustang for just one thing — revenge! Revenge on the people who had him thrown in jail.

HELL RIDERS
Steve Mensing

Wade Walker's kid brother, Duane, was locked up in the Silver City jail facing a rope at dawn. Wade was a ruthless outlaw, but he was smart, and he had vowed to have his brother out of jail before morning!

DESERT OF THE DAMNED
Nelson Nye

The law was after him for the murder of a marshal — a murder he didn't commit. Breen was after him for revenge — and Breen wouldn't stop at anything . . . blackmail, a frameup . . . or murder.

DAY OF THE COMANCHEROS
Steven C. Lawrence

Their very name struck terror into men's hearts — the Comancheros, a savage army of cutthroats who swept across Texas, leaving behind a bloodstained trail of robbery and murder.

SUNDANCE: SILENT ENEMY
John Benteen

A lone crazed Cheyenne was on a personal war path. They needed to pit one man against one crazed Indian. That man was Sundance.

LASSITER
Jack Slade

Lassiter wasn't the kind of man to listen to reason. Cross him once and he'll hold a grudge for years to come — if he let you live that long.

LAST STAGE TO GOMORRAH
Barry Cord

Jeff Carter, tough ex-riverboat gambler, now had himself a horse ranch that kept him free from gunfights and card games. Until Sturvesant of Wells Fargo showed up.

McALLISTER ON THE COMANCHE CROSSING
Matt Chisholm

The Comanche, McAllister owes them a life — and the trail is soaked with the blood of the men who had tried to outrun them before.

QUICK-TRIGGER COUNTRY
Clem Colt

Turkey Red hooked up with Curly Bill Graham's outlaw crew. But wholesale murder was out of Turk's line, so when range war flared he bucked the whole border gang alone . . .

CAMPAIGNING
Jim Miller

Ambushed on the Santa Fe trail, Sean Callahan is saved by two Indian strangers. But there'll be more lead and arrows flying before the band join Kit Carson against the Comanches.

GUNSLINGER'S RANGE
Jackson Cole

Three escaped convicts are out for revenge. They won't rest until they put a bullet through the head of the dirty snake who locked them behind bars.

RUSTLER'S TRAIL
Lee Floren

Jim Carlin knew he would have to stand up and fight because he had staked his claim right in the middle of Big Ike Outland's best grass.

THE TRUTH ABOUT SNAKE RIDGE
Marshall Grover

The troubleshooters came to San Cristobal to help the needy. For Larry and Stretch the turmoil began with a brawl and then an ambush.

WOLF DOG RANGE
Lee Floren

Will Ardery would stop at nothing, unless something stopped him first — like a bullet from Pete Manly's gun.

DEVIL'S DINERO
Marshall Grover

Plagued by remorse, a rich old reprobate hired the Texas Troubleshooters to deliver a fortune in greenbacks to each of his victims.

GUNS OF FURY
Ernest Haycox

Dane Starr, alias Dan Smith, wanted to close the door on his past and hang up his guns, but people wouldn't let him.

DONOVAN
Elmer Kelton

Donovan was supposed to be dead. Uncle Joe Vickers had fired off both barrels of a shotgun into the vicious outlaw's face as he was escaping from jail. Now Uncle Joe had been shot — in just the same way.

CODE OF THE GUN
Gordon D. Shirreffs

MacLean came riding home, with saddle tramp written all over him, but sewn in his shirt-lining was an Arizona Ranger's star.

GAMBLER'S GUN LUCK
Brett Austen

Gamblers seldom live long. Parker was a hell of a gambler. It was his life — or his death . . .

ORPHAN'S PREFERRED
Jim Miller

Sean Callahan answers the call of the Pony Express and fights Indians and outlaws to get the mail through.

DAY OF THE BUZZARD
T. V. Olsen

All Val Penmark cared about was getting the men who killed his wife.

THE MANHUNTER
Gordon D. Shirreffs

Lee Kershaw knew that every Rurale in the territory was on the lookout for him. But the offer of $5,000 in gold to find five small pieces of leather was too good to turn down.

RIFLES ON THE RANGE
Lee Floren

Doc Mike and the farmer stood there alone between Smith and Watson. There was this moment of stillness, and then the roar would start. And somebody would die . . .

HARTIGAN
Marshall Grover

Hartigan had come to Cornerstone to die. He chose the time and the place, and Main Street became a battlefield.

SUNDANCE: OVERKILL
John Benteen

When a wealthy banker's daughter was kidnapped by the Cheyenne, he offered Sundance $10,000 to rescue the girl.